The Problem Solver:

❧ Drug Lords ☙

Ron Mueller

Drug Lords

The Problem Solver: Book Two

✎ *Drug Lords* ✎

Ron Mueller

Around the World Publishing LLC
Cincinnati, Ohio 45242

This book is a work of fiction. Names, characters, places, and incidents either are products of the author's imagination or are used fictitiously. Any resemblance to actual events or locales or persons, living or dead, is entirely coincidental.

Drug Lords ©

ISBN 13: 978-1-68223-980-3

Distributed by Ingram
Cover Picture by Bruce Rolff @Dreamstime
Cover Design by Ron Mueller

vi

<u>*Dedication*</u>

To those fighting to reduce the drug flow.

<u>Drug Lords</u>

<u>Introduction</u>

We will never stop the flow of drugs coming into this country as long as there are customer wanting to buy it.

Prohibition of a specific good has never worked. This is true for the oldest profession, liquor and now drugs. If there is a pull, the flow will continue.

Many countermeasures to the drug flow have been proposed. It will take a combination of all of them to make any significant impact.

The biggest impact would come about if there were no customers.

The next biggest would be that drugs would be so cheap and the margin so low that it would not be a very attractive business.

This is the story of an action directly targeting the primary businessmen that manage the drug flow logistics. They are family men and women. They are a part of the fabric of the society in which they exist.

They are also ruthless to those opposing them and even more ruthless to their competitors.

Their lives are always on the line. They take many lives but often theirs are taken as well.

The financial rewards are great. The price for these "businessmen" often exceeds the reward.

<u>*Drug Lords*</u>

<u>*1 Assignment*</u>

*T*he kids were now all out of college.

Ella and family were established in Georgia.

Matt was a programmer.

Sean was now established in California and had a partner.

Lesley and he missed having them around the house. They visited often but the two of them had more house than he had ever wanted.

Ian had come to accept and enjoy the space. He still thought of it as decadent, but he had become accustomed to it and was relaxed and enjoyed the decadent life that he lived.

He spent a great deal of time in his library office.

Massive bookshelves held hundreds of the classics and many of his own writings. He had stopped collecting books. He had transitioned into what he called the world of his children. He was a computer nerd. His use of the internet and Google had become common.

He still loved to periodically pick out one of the books and sit down to read but the majority of his time was on the keyboard of his computer.

His new iPhone vibrating in his pocket had sent a shiver down his back and raised the hairs on the back of his neck.

He knew the message was no coincidence. As he watched the CNN news cast about the beheading of the policemen in Mexico, the news caster had called for someone to resolve the terrorism going on in Mexico.

He knew these words were meant for him.

"Call" was the text on his personal iPhone that had come up right after the news cast.

He knew immediately this would be an assignment that he would not want. He also knew this was not a call to be made from his personal phone.

He thought back to two previous calls.

One had sent him into the heart of Russia to stop or delay the development of an intelligent missile system.

The other call had sent him to the Gaza Strip to eliminate three terrorists being exchanged for one Israeli soldier.

His job was to solve problems that could not be addressed in a politically correct manner.

His targets often ceased to exist.

He usually received his assignments directly from a news broadcast when the announcer asked, "Who can lead us to a solution to this problem?" or some other similar phrase. Such a statement would cause him to replay that segment of the news multiple times.

Usually, he was on his own to respond. He seldom got any directions from his handler. He seemed to correctly respond to most of the calls. He knew this because his bank account always received an appropriate influx.

He sat down in the thickly padded desk chair and opened the bottom left desk drawer of his desk. At the very back was a combination lock box. He pulled it out and placed it in front of him. He keyed in the five digits on the touch lock, lifted the box lid and took out the phone. It was the older phone version that did not have a GPS module. It had only one number stored in its memory. Ian pushed the dial button.

He knew he was a problem-solving junkie. He loved to pit himself against the "bad" guy. He had survived for more than thirty years at a calling that normally meant a short life. He was alive because of his low key, almost invisible way of solving these special problems. When he was in the field his senses were at their height.

He could smell and taste trouble.

His premonition for trouble was mind blowing.

Several times he had gone from plan a to plan b to plan c as the action unfolded. He had always wondered what would happen when he ran out of plans.

He swiveled in his chair and looked out the windows directly at the tennis courts. It was dimly lit by one of the security lights that was on the far side.

He could faintly hear the water fall from the hot tub to the pool on the other side of the family room as he put in the ear buds and then plugged them into the phone. His mouth was dry, and he wished he had his normal tall twenty-ounce thermal mug of Pellegrino and ice.

He hesitated a moment, let his mind relax and then made the phone call.

The silence just before the phone began to Bing, Bing, Bing as it connected was disconcerting. He always imagined this as a call to hell and the person answering it as the devil himself.

Only Lesley was aware of this alternate world he lived in. The rest of his family did not have a clue. He had to fight the overwhelming urge to hang up. He did not want to get into a long, protracted assignment. He was ready to retire from the role of being the on-call problem-solver.

This was not a movie.

There would be no flash of light to erase his memories.

His memories were clear.

His life was the yin and yang, of good and evil, of dark and light.

He had willingly participated in both worlds.

Ian thought again of the two lives he lived.

They were polar opposites and in both-worlds he was the problem-solver.

"It's been a long time," said a familiar voice on the other end of the line.

"Not long enough," Ian replied as he thought about his last assignment that had taken him into the Heart of Russia.

"This assignment will be tough and perhaps long. We have arranged for a leave of absence from your company. We will provide all the help that you ask for. Your account will cover whatever you need."

He thought about his bottomless million-dollar offshore account. On one assignment he had purchased a multi-million-dollar yacht with no questions asked. The yacht had ended up somewhere in the government system.

"Your assignment is to take out the top leader of every drug cartel in Mexico."

"You have got to be crazy. Me and what army," he snapped back?

He was holding onto the edge of his desk as he experienced the world turning black. He was seeing everything in front of him through a tiny white hole that was slowly growing smaller.

He was about to pass out.

He took several deep breaths and slowly the lights came back on. He had a metallic taste in his mouth, and he felt cold all over.

"We know this is a tough one and we have assembled the strongest and best support team you can possibly want. We have also made arrangements to get you included in several key organizations that will give you ample cover."

He remained silent. Backup team! Ample cover! Who the hell did they think he was?

"Great to talk with you, Good Luck, and may the force be with you," the voice on the other end said in a formal manner.

Then the phone went dead.

He looked at the silent phone in his hand.

Who the hell do they think I am, superman?

He slowly put the phone into the box, locked it and put it in the back of the desk drawer.

He got up and slowly walked to the kitchen where he knew he would find a cup of coffee.

He knew that he would accept the challenge. There was some part of him that loved to pit himself against the bad guy. This assignment would be the ultimate challenge.

He wondered whether this would be his "swan song." He hoped not, he had visions of sitting in front of his fireplace with Leslie snuggling next to him reading.

His mind was already kicking into high gear. He could feel his heart beating a little faster and he could smell the leather of his chair as his sense of smell sharpened.

He thought that he could taste the mountain air in the coffee he was drinking.

This primordial reaction to a challenge that would involve eliminating his opponent always came as a surprise. His energy level immediately hit a new high and he knew it would stay high until the letdown that always came at the end of an assignment.

"Do any of these supporting team members have names," Ian had inquired?

"No and you know better than to ask. So, I take it that you have accepted and are ready to go," the devil's voice had responded.

"You knew the answer before I returned your called," Ian had replied.

He knew he would need a workplace outside of his home to prepare for this assignment. In his mind there would be at least six to eight months of research and planning.

He went online to find office space that would be close to home but secluded enough that he would not be noticed.

His search took him to a twelve hundred square foot, second floor office area with windows around three sides of the room. The windows were modern, triple layered gas filled. The floor space was for an open office layout.

He laughed as he thought about the open office layout aspect. There would be no one else but he and his computer in the office.

But it seemed to be what he needed.

He called the listing realtor and made an appointment to meet him at the location and walk the office space.

The tree lined parking area, the well-kept green area, and the office space itself made for a very comfortable work arrangement. After the walk through, Ian bargained with the realtor on the length and the price of the lease. He got eggshell colored, simulated wood vertical hanging blinds for the windows thrown in as part of the contract.

He would have had the blinds put in anyway, but he wanted the realtor to feel as if he was doing his job and that the customer was truly trying to get the best deal possible.

Three days later, he carried in seven flip charts and easel stands. The four-by-eight-foot walnut desk and large black leather office chair was scheduled for delivery between twelve and two. He had also ordered several office tables and half a dozen chairs.

He would pick up his Dell 36-inch, 128 TB hard drive, computer and monitor at the store after the desk arrived. It was an all-in-one computer where the monitor and the computer was one unit. This would be the computer to search the internet and to research his intended targets.

Ian walked around the perimeter of the office as he thought about how to lay out his meager office furniture.

He was on his second walk and about ready to put up his easels when he realized his thinking was antiquated.

He had envisioned using the seven easels as the media to organize the information and to display the plans for the interaction with each of the drug cartels.

He realized he was thinking in yesterday's terms. He realized that he should be setting up a separate computer systems for each cartel.

His personal goal was to survive this problem-solving assignment.

To do so he would need to be at the top of his game.

He scolded himself and told himself he had better sharpen his thinking and shape up fast.

He could not be a fossil he needed to leverage all the latest technology.

He immediately called the store where he had bought the Dell and asked for seven similar but lower end computers. The store clerk said he had just what he needed. They would all be all-in-one computers and he would send them along with the one that was already scheduled to be delivered, and everything would be put on one bill.

He interpreted the enthusiasm in the clerk's voice ensured that he would get what was needed.

All the equipment arrived as scheduled. He had the deliverers put the computers on the tables he had set up around the room. Afterwards he set everything up and made sure everything worked.

He knew he had to create the connection from each cartel focused computer to a central control computer.

He called his on-line support group and asked them to guide him in setting up an in-office network.

With step-by-step guidance, he was able to set up the network in one afternoon. The internal network was not online. Only his main computer would connect to the global internet, and the main computer would not connect to his internal network. His internal network would be totally isolated.

Seven-thirty the next morning, he parked his ten-year-old, dark green sedan with a black leather interior that his Leslie made him park immediately in the garage and close the door when he arrived home.

This was one item he had refused to upgrade. He always bought used cars and refused to drive any of the luxury cars that were par for his neighborhood.

It was one thing to have lucked out in buying the grand palace they called home, but it was another to compete with the neighbors to see who could drive the most expensive car to show who had the most money.

Bullshit! was what went through his mind each time he attended a neighborhood party and listened to the conversations of condescending, haughty, pompous attitudes of superior mental midgets with their hand waving and the rolling of eyes as various groups gathered to impress each other.

The office building was one of several in the industrial park. All seemed to be duplicates of each other and had a row of evergreen bushes around their perimeter.

The gold number printed in the horizontal glass across the top of the doors to his office building provided the only means of telling the difference between the other six buildings in the complex.

Maple trees were the dominant species surrounding each parking area. Two rows of six-inch diameter trees ran lengthwise across each lot.

Except at high noon the parking areas were always shaded. His parking area, specifically meant to be for his building, usually had one car parked in it. He was the only current renter of floor space in his building. He had the entire floor, but he was the only person working there.

He, carrying his light brown leather briefcase that featured a flap buckled on one side, walked slowly toward the office. He pressed his key-fob and listened for the beep of the car horn letting him know that it was locked.

"Stupid habit" went through his mind. There was nothing in the car worth stealing, he thought as he looked up through the heavily leaved branches of the maples to a clear blue morning sky.

His family had no clue as to where his current work location was. Long ago he had given up having a landline office phone. All calls, whether business or personal, came to the same phone. He had made sure to turn off his GPS and turned off the sharing location feature.

It was time to get started on the overall plan for this assignment. After that he would begin the research into each individual cartel.

The parking lot ended about one hundred feet from the building's double doors. He stepped up from the black top surface to the worn, heavily pebbled cement walk that was obviously sealed in some plastic sealer. The pebbles were preventing an otherwise deteriorating surface from getting any worse. The sealer gave the walk an old nostalgic look.

The newly planted yellow and gold marigold flowers edging the sidewalk on the building side provided an elegant touch to an otherwise plain office area. He looked down past the two additional buildings in this section of the park and was pleased with the harmony the flowers, trees and bushes provided.

"Damn," he exclaimed as the right-hand door remained closed when he tried pulling it open. The left-hand door responded easily to his pull.

It seemed to him that every double glass door always had one side locked. Why have two doors if one was always locked? He would need to post a big arrow on the locked door pointing to the open one to remind him which side to use.

He noted that the bottom floor of the building was currently empty. He hoped it would remain that way.

The six-foot-wide, grey, and black granite step slabs held in place by a black steel frame went up the left side of the entrance. Halfway up, the stairs made a ninety degree turn and continued to the second floor. The second-floor landing area and the hallway leading back to the Men's and Ladies restroom matched the granite of the steps.

It was clear that these buildings had been upscale offices at one time. They were still in good condition and well kept. Businesses had moved out as the business expansion had moved from an eastward expansion to a southward one that made its way to the Airport.

Once at the top of the stairs Ian's office area was immediately to the right. He put the key fob up to the lock and heard the opening click.

The doorknob turned effortlessly, and he stepped in and closed and locked the door behind him.

On the far end of the office area, was a dark walnut desk that faced the entrance. It had a very large computer screen standing on it. This was his search, find and research center.

About ten feet in front of it was a duplicate desk that was the command center for the internal computer network. In front of that desk, fanned out across the room in a semi-circle, were tables with another set of computers with their screens all facing the center.

This lay out took up half of the office floor space. The back area was what he considered the work area. He had no people but a boat load of technology. He thought of the semi-circle of computers as his technological employees.

These were employees that got no salary or medical benefits, and could voice no complaints, another words perfect employees.

The first half of the floor was appointed with a large oriental rug, a couch and a large recliner bracketed by two lamps on square walnut stands. This part of the office area looked back toward the two command desks and was clearly a rest and relax area.

In the front left corner of the office, behind the recliner, a refreshment center held a stainless-steel refrigerator, a microwave, a small counter top oven and a coffee or tea maker.

The recliner area was his relaxation and thinking area.

Today he would be focusing on getting an overall plan outlined.

He needed to come up with a plan that contained three key elements: A research element,

The guiding plan, and

Flawless execution detail.

The first was the most critical.

The second essential to returning to his good life.

The third critical to achieving his mission of coming home alive.

He walked slowly across the office area looking for any proof that his support team had come in overnight to fulfill his request to get his office shielded from broadcasting beyond the office walls.

He was worried about two major technical issues. The first concern was the ability for web sites he researched to track him to his computer. The second concern was not to have his internal wireless network broadcasting beyond the perimeter of the office area.

He felt that needed to maintain a high degree of secrecy.

He immediately noticed the vertical silver wire that went down each of the vertical blinds. The wires were connected at the top of the blinds with small delicate silver chains. He walked up close and could see that the entire office area was now behind a grounded metal mesh shield.

He smiled as he took in the hip designer feel it gave his office.

"Well, done team," he thought as he finished walking around the perimeter.

As he approached his main computer, he noticed that the screen was on and had a message clarifying the six-layer computer isolation from the internet. The cookies he was worried about would never reach the shielded level occupied by his computer.

"Well, done again," he thought.

Ian sat down and leaned back into his chair.

He pressed start on his computer and the message the team had left disappeared, and his blank screen desktop appeared.

He opened his briefcase and took out a dozen 18 terra bite memory sticks and put them into the top drawer. He put his old cherished brief case to the side of the desk and then pulled up a detailed map of North America on the computer and saved it onto one of the memory sticks.

He pulled out the memory stick and walked around to the desk immediately in front of him, turned on that computer and transferred the map into the master plan folder.

He focused on the US-Mexico border and tried to contemplate how he might approach his problem-solving assignment.

Starting on the Gulf of Mexico at Brownsville, Texas seemed to be as good as any place. He would then proceed westward along the border to San Diego. He knew there were several cartels along the border and then one in Tijuana.

He would continue south down the Pacific coast side around the tip of the California peninsula and back to Mexico City.

He drew the path across the map.

He took it all in and let it flow through his mind.

It seemed to make sense to him.

He immediately felt a sense of relief as he got his first piece of the plan saved onto a file. In the old days, he would have saved the paper flip chart. Saving it to a file did not seem to have the same beefy feel to it but he knew that it was a more flexible way to manage the information.

He now felt ready to begin the investigation of the drug cartels themselves.

He took a time out to get a cup of tea. This was his preferred caffeine source. Just about any tea would do, but Jasmine and Chamomile were his two mainstays but name almost any tea and he would at least have one sealed bag of it. He always used a teaspoon of local honey, that he bought from a former colleague, to sweeten the tea.

From his easy chair he took in the work area in front of him.

He could have located both computers on the same desk, but he wanted a physical reminder and a physical separator to emphasize the split between his research and his planning.

He could not afford even a momentary lapse in the separation of information.

His internal network needed to remain totally isolated. Each of the internal network computers would hold specific information for one of the targeted cartels.

He knew his life depended on his ability to compartmentalize and separate the information that he was generating about each cartel.

Sitting in his break area sipping on his tea served to give him time to think about his next steps.

He eventually would envision, think through in detail and when appropriate act out every action he planned to take. The break area was as important to him as the two research computers and the internal computer network.

He knew the most important computer in the room was the organic one shielded by his thick skull.

As fractured and damaged as his brain might be, it was what had kept him alive through the many problem-solving sessions he had been on.

Even the dark part of his mind that often taunted him cooperated in making sure he remained alive.

It was time to begin his research into the drug cartels and learn about their leaders. This was where deep understanding of the situation was important. He would need to see and understand aspects of the operations of the cartels that others had either missed or ignored.

His approach needed to go beyond the facts and needed to give him the knowledge that would allow him to execute his plan and live to take the next step.

Utilizing the resources he had at hand, he would study each cartel separately and as deeply as he could.

He activated one of his special GPS free phones and called the support number of his team. He put in a request for all drug cartel information available in any US or ally government data bases.

He then went to Google and began traveling the streets of Matamoros and regions controlled by the Gulf Cartel. After spending most of the afternoon understanding the history and the current operation of the Gulf Cartel, the infighting and positioning of the various members of the cartel the futility of the assignment he had taken on became clear.

He would strike a blow to the leadership of the Gulf Cartel, but it was a hydra with multiple heads, and it would most likely just grow another. His strike on this cartel would be noticed but no matter what leader he took out, there would be another one to immediately rise up to take his place.

He stored his notes onto the thumb drive, stood up and walked to the internal network computer in front of him. He stored the information into the first computer. He made a paper tent label from an eight-by-eleven-inch sheet of paper and with a big black marker wrote "Gulf Cartel." He put the label on the left hand most computer in the arc of computers before him.

He would give each of his electronic lackeys' appropriate names.

It was time for a break and another cup of tea.

After that each additional cartel would get the same deep scrutiny. He allowed for one week of deep study for each cartel.

He continued with his research and planning. He prepared the entire problem-solving circuit.

Then he envisioned his action at each problem-solving location. As he did this, he made a list of the tools, materials, or weapons he would need.

After reviewing and finalizing the materials he requested his support team to obtain and position the materials in the proximity of where each problem-solving session would be.

He walked through multiple scenarios at each problem-solving locality.

He was leaving nothing to chance. He planned for success, but he also tried to imagine what could go wrong and planned for that scenario as well. He wondered what went through the minds of his support team. They certainly must be thinking he was at the edge of falling of the reality cliff.

He concluded a lot could go wrong. He was going in alone against people practiced in the art of eliminating their enemy. It was clear to him that even the Mexican and US governments had stayed clear of a direct confrontation with the various drug cartels.

He had no illusions about the enormous money, power, and influence that the cartels had and that they often flexed their power when confronted by an adversary.

He would be on his own. His success was predicated on his ability to remain a ghost. He would need to remain invisible and move faster than the cartel leaders recognized or figured out the pattern of his problem-solving.

<u>2 Matamoros-The Gulf Cartel</u>

*I*an learned that the Gulf Cartel was one of the oldest of the seven major cartels on his list. It had participated in smuggling booze into the US during the Prohibition era. Later it turned to drug smuggling, collecting protection money from businesses, engaged in human transport, and kidnapping. It had solid connections and affiliations throughout the US and Europe.

It was clear to Ian that it was a sophisticated operation. It emulated the big companies on Wall Street. Many of the cartels even had a board of directors.

He thought that was appropriate. They trafficked in drugs and Wall Street trafficked in money.

Some people partook of both.

Both were led by people only interested in grabbing more money.

One had lobbyists working to ensure their money grab looked legal and the other simply ignored the law and did what they wanted.

The Gulf Cartel's leadership was split between two factions currently working together to control the same territory and to fight off the Los Zetas cartel operating in Nuevo Laredo.

He thoroughly studied both factions and with the help of his nameless support team he had identified a protection collection route that one of the leaders consistently followed. The target Ian selected was not the top leader of the Cartel but was a key member on the Board.

He was the unlucky target.

The location of the top leader was currently a mystery. He solved it but decided that the location made it an even more risky one than he could imagine.

Utilizing Google map street view, he drove the same route, taken by this unlucky leader, multiple times, on his visits to various businesses.

Then he slowly and carefully studied the route and decided on the place where he would solve the problem.

The stucco multicolored buildings on each side, with their iron grated windows and doors presented the dichotomy of the environment. Here lived cheerful, hardworking people fearful of the desperate, the jobless, the hungry and the drug runners.

Here lived people who enjoyed sitting outside of restaurants and coffee shops but who were currently under the control of the drug cartels and under the control of the many corrupt policemen. These were mostly good, god-fearing people wanting to live in peace and raise their children.

But the honest policemen had their heads cut off! Honest people stayed in the shadows and tried to stay out of the eyes of the cartels.

He stopped and studied a place that was called, "*The English Coffee Shop.*" It featured a rather French like coffee shop layout with white tablecloths over black iron tables with matching black iron chairs. On the sidewalk there were several tables.

A night shot of the street showed the lights coming down from the steel bar covered windows on the second floor affirming them as apartments or homes for the shop owners or renters. This was by all accounts a vibrant neighborhood.

The building opposite the café where the actual explosion would take place presented a clean, red brick wall with no windows. This was a relief to him. His goal was to have no collateral injuries.

After three more examinations of the route, he knew what he would do.

During his research of Matamoros, he saw the ads for a robot fight tournament. He put in an inquiry to his support team to see if he could somehow get on one of the robot fight teams. It would serve as a perfect cover.

A few days later, as he sat at his primary office desk, he got a call on one of his support phones.

"You are now a member of the University of Illinois Fighting Robot Wedge team. You are their last-minute design engineer replacing their "sick" team member, call to get acquainted with the fighting robot team," was the message.

He dialed the number he had been given and waited for someone to pick-up on the other end.

This is Trip Masters, your fight design engineer, he stated his name as someone answered the phone.

"Great to hear from you Trip. I am Dr. John Newton, but I am called Dr. J by my team. My team and I have been working hard to get to the top for a long time

You better be good.

The team that beat us has a unit almost identical to ours entered in the Matamoros competition.

Our design engineer was tops.

You better be good," Dr. J finished his long introduction.

"When can you get to Champaign-Urbana to help us finalize our entry," he asked?

"I can be there in about a day. This seems to be rather close to the competition to be finalizing the designing of your unit," Ian replied as he realized they wanted some real engineering design work from him and thought he actually had robot design expertise.

Dr. J agreed that the finalizing of the design was very late, but they were worried about what they had heard about the improvements by their competition. The team wanted to reassess their current design.

He let Lesley know that he was going to the University of Illinois for a few days. This was, he told her, in preparation for his upcoming trip.

Lesley smiled and joked that it was good to see him seeking to improve his mind.

He drove to the main U of I campus the next day and put up for the night at a local B&B.

Early the next morning, he parked his rental in an almost empty parking lot and began his walk across the campus.

The chh, chh, chh, of the sprinklers and the cool breeze on his face invaded his wandering thoughts.

The dark aroma of the coffee and the sharp strands of light from the sun peeking over the building at the other end of the campus mall began to penetrate his waking mind.

The mall seemed to have been newly renovated and landscaped. The broad sidewalk was a combination of reddish-brown brick laid out in a herring bone pattern surrounded by a rectangular cement frame. Every square had at least one brick in a center square with the name of the person or family that had donated money to fund the renovation. There was space for new donation bricks to be added.

Young eight-foot-high maple trees with tinted hardy orange mums planted at their base were equally spaced around the mall on both sides of the walk. Most trees had an accompanying plaque dedicating the tree to a loved one.

His mind imagined the day these young trees would create an arch over the walk. He could see the fall yellow, orange, and red colors the trees would display. It was a beautiful mental image for the slightly anemic looking young trees.

The Mall, about the size of three end to end football fields, was highlighted with three, equally spaced, round, rose gardens. These gardens and the thick green grass gave a long-term promise of upcoming elegance.

The first big decision of the morning was whether to go clockwise or counterclockwise to reach the building at the far end. The young black policewoman coming toward him crystalized his choice and he walked slowly toward her.

They both stopped when a biker riding the same path enthusiastically let them know she was coming through.

At that moment, the chirping of the birds replaced the chh, chh, chh of the sprinklers as they stopped and the warmth of the sun penetrated the black tee shirt Ian was wearing.

Morning had arrived in full force.

He took in the fresh spit polished uniform and the confidence displayed by the young policewoman. This was probably her first professional job, and it was clear by her thrown back shoulders and smooth confident walk she was proud of her job.

The aroma that accompanied a slow sip of his coffee prepared him for this first encounter of the day.

"Hi, I'm looking for Dr. John Newton," he said in greeting.

"Oh, you must mean Dr. J. Are you the new high-powered fight design engineer I heard him talking about at the coffee shop?"

He's counting on you to make a difference.

The team has come in second in the last two years.

They really want to break that cycle," she rapidly replied.

Pointing to the building at the far end of the mall, she instructed him to go in the first door, go down into the basement. Turn left and then follow the hall until he got to the first set of double doors.

She told him to knock loudly since the door was key card locked and the folks inside sometimes made an awful racket.

He thanked her and walked leisurely toward the building.

The hallway back to the double doors was dimly lit and had a moldy smell.

He wondered how an award-winning team could be relegated to the conditions he was walking through.

The keycard lock guarded a brushed stainless-steel door. Its clean fresh appearance put it at odds with the darker, more worn surroundings.

It seemed to be the right door, so he knocked.

"Welcome to our private playground," Dr. J said as he pulled him in and closed the door.

The transition was amazing. He entered a bright laboratory style room with a stainless-steel countertop all the way around the outside walls and three six by six-foot stainless-steel islands at its center.

The room had a high ceiling and there were numerous machine tools, welders, and metal working equipment situated around the room.

On the center table roughly six by six foot in size was what Ian took to be the fighting wedge robot.

"That is the robot and let me introduce the team that thought of it, designed it, built it and took it to many wins," Dr. J said.

He noticed that Dr. J kept one hand on the robot as if it were a bible as he made the introductions.

"Marty is the electronics genius that designed the control circuits. Samantha is the machine and metal working specialist that cuts, shapes and welds. Henry is the main robot operator. His deft hands and mind have guided our wedge to many victories.

I am the back-up operator. Sam is the team's logistics and set up support," Dr. J continued.

"Thanks for filling in for our design engineer. News has it that his father is dying, and he needed to stay with his family."

"I was told you were the world's best robot fighter design engineer.   How come we haven't seen you at any of the competitions," Dr. J inquired?

It was clear to Ian that their design engineer had been offered a significant incentive to have a dying father. He had experienced a similar situation in several previous problem-solving assignments. He knew that in this case, if he were going to lie, it would need to be a big one.

"You haven't heard of me because I play with robots designed not to compete with other robots but designed to kill anything it is assigned to kill," he lied with a straight face.

"Let's study the plans of your fighting robot and list all the fatal weaknesses that we can," he moved the team immediately into an action that would highlight what they knew were fatal flaws of their design.

He pulled a white board over and opened the black marker pen. He listened and put up the weaknesses the team identified. He kept the list to the left side.

Then he began to ask the questions that each identified flaw caused him to ask.

"You know that if you get turned over, you are in trouble. Why not make both sides operate the same," was his first suggestion?

"Your current strategy is to outlast the opponent. Why not kill him immediately," was his next question?

"You count on one of your team members to visually manipulate the robot during battle. Why not give the robot the ability to act and activate its defenses based on the movement and position of its robot opponent," was his final question?

At first there were some defensive replies. Then the team got into identifying improvements to the new ideas.

It was clear to him why the team did so well in competitions.

One of the team pointed out the limited amount of time before the tournament.

He counter that he understood that it would be a monumental challenge but to continue doing the same would be to have the same results as in previous years.

He asked if they wanted to be the world champions.

"I understand the challenge. I will work with Samantha on building the new shell for the robot. You work on the controls and intelligence. Dr. J can work on the weapons," he countered.

He looked at the team.

Dr. J. looked back at him then turned to the team and simply said, "Let's do it."

He was pleased with himself. He had no clue about robotics, but he knew how to envision and empower teams.

He stepped in toward Dr. J and put out his hand palm down. Dr. J understood immediately and put his hand on top of Ian's. The rest of the team followed and in unison the whole team shouted loudly, "Let's do it."

By Friday after spending twenty hours each day and eating in the lab, testing each item as they went, the team was standing around the large table admiring the new robot.

"Look at this beauty," Dr. J said as he stroked the low slung, three-inch-thick plain stainless-steel disc. Samantha had polished the shiny stainless-steel alien spacecraft looking robot to almost a mirror finish.

There was nothing to prevent the opponent from turning the disc over. The tactic of lifting and turning the opponent over was a common attack practice.

This robot wanted that to occur.

Once contact with the opponent was made, the robot drove spikes into the opponent and then climbed on to it. If the spikes did not take hold, they retracted and the whole unit allowed itself to be turned over. The other side was exactly the same, so it waited for the opponent to try the turnover attack again.

However, at the peak of the second flip, the side opposite the opponent launched a thin cable to lasso the opponent. If the lasso caught the opponent, the entire robot would pull itself on top of the opponent and ooze out super glue. The units would be bonded, and the robot began its boring and laser cutting.

The boring and laser cutting would create very small holes. Acid was then injected into the opponent and the party was soon over.

"This is diabolical. How did you ever think of all of this," Dr. J asked as he looked at Ian?

Ian pointed out that he had not suggested any of what was now called nasty and killer ideas. "I only asked questions. You all piled the nasty on," he said quietly.

"We did in fact do that, but we would never have thought of all of this in one package," Henry commented.

"What are we going to call this beast," Samantha asked as she lovingly put her hand on the polished metal surface of the robot.

"Why not *Muerte de Norte,* Death from the North," Ian suggested.

"That is a great name," the rest of the team commented in unison.

"I am going to etch it on the surface of both sides of our robot," Samantha said as she got out her Dremel tool and put a small grinding fixture in it.

"It's time for our road trip to Matamoras and victory. Let's get Muerte de Norte loaded up. We leave tomorrow," Dr. J declared.

"I need to get a couple of things done before I go. I will meet you at the hotel in Matamoros," he said as he got up and headed for the door.

He had discovered the University only paid for shared hotel rooms. He needed to have a private room for himself and decided that all of them should have the same status. He asked his support team to call ahead to the hotel and make the arrangements and to rent the best rooms.

He looked back at the stainless-steel door and then turned to walk up the stairs out to the U of I mall. This time he took the right path around and walked slowly through the meager shade of the young maples as he admired the three rose gardens in the middle. The mall had a few students either hurrying to their classes, sitting on the benches, or sitting out directly on the grass.

He wondered how many of them funded the drug lords he was on the way to punish for providing what the customers wanted.

He returned home before beginning his problem-solving journey in Matamoros. Once he left home it would be several months before he would be able to return.

The two days home evaporated quicker than a window spray on a car's hot glass windshield. He knew his return home would only take as long as a wait in the emergency room when you only had a cold. He knew from experience it would seem longer than he anticipated.

He contacted the support team and gave them instructions on cleaning and emptying the planning office.

Lesley seemed to know that he was on one of his special problem-solving trips. She whispered that she loved him, wished him luck, and told him to be careful.

The sun was halfway on its daily journey across the sky in front of the house and the tree shadows were getting to their smallest stature with clouds seemingly hovering over them like whipped cream on a green tea sundae as he gave Lesley a hug and kiss and walked slowly toward the cab.

The taxi driver was standing with the trunk open, ready for the one blue green medium-sized suitcase he had packed.

Always a light traveler, he never carried more than the one suitcase and his briefcase. Periodically he would choose a slightly larger suitcase for the longer trips or a smaller one for day trips. In this case, he had chosen the medium one because he had prearranged materials and clothes to be strategically located along the entire problem-solving trip.

He felt the surge of energy he always experienced at the beginning of an assignment. The forty-five-minute trip to the airport evaporated in the intense mix of the thoughts and scenarios he played out in his mind. All of his plans were now in his head.

The computer he carried was clean. He knew this because it was fresh out of the box, and he had yet to set it up.

The driver's announcement of their arrival caught him by surprise. He automatically paid and tipped and proceeded to baggage check in.

Ian was glad to see that there was only a light crowd. He had armed his new identity with the appropriate road warrior miles and a diamond medallion status. He went through security in the express lane and was soon on board the tram to the B concourse.

Starbucks was on the right at the top of the escalator leading up into the concourse. He stopped and bought a double espresso and then poured in a healthy amount of cream. He seldom bought his coffee from Starbucks, but he was now playing the part of a typical businessman. The cup in his hand was symbolic, it was the sign of a seasoned road warrior.

He was dressed in business casual. His carry on was only his briefcase and the Starbucks latte.

He wanted to be seen as the high mileage business jerk who gets the aisle seat and gets to board early and suck up the overhead space.

On this trip he had bought the ticket via the internet, under a fictitious name with a credit card that was closed shortly after paying for the ticket.

He loved watching the folks as they got on the plane.

Every mood possible was displayed.

He especially wondered about those folks who came on looking like sour milk or seemed to exude dislike for all those around them.

Then there were the blissfully happy ones or the ones he would not have wanted to play poker with. He always joked with the kids or the mother's struggling to control several at one time. He always wondered how mothers were able to remain sane on such travels.

The flight to San Antonio was uneventful. It gave him plenty of time to go over every action he would take on the first trip across the border into Mexico. He felt reassured for the solid cover of the robot tournament. It made him more invisible than he would otherwise have been.

The intense week at the University had truly bonded him with the team. They provided the same emotional lift that the smell of a young puppy gave him. They exuded wonderment and positive feeling about their future. He hoped that they would reach the peak they were aiming for.

Once the plane stopped at the gate, he immediately stood up and got his bag from the overhead. There was a wait, while sequentially each individual got up, reclaimed their bag, and then proceeded down the aisle. He was content to just stand and wait. He hated to sit in the small seats.

Once out of the plane, he walked briskly toward the exit and the cab stand. He took a cab to the downtown San Antonio river walk.

He walked down the steps to the flagstone walk that bordered the most domesticated river he could imagine. It no longer had river banks but was walled in and reminded him of a long flowing swimming pool bound on two sides with cement, brick and stone walls and lined with gardens of flowers and trees.

The completely domesticated river reminded him of a farm boy in a tuxedo at an elite debutante ball in South Georgia. Both made him uncomfortable. Both were totally foreign and out of place.

Standing below the palm trees competing with tall, large live oaks to provide shade from the uncompromising heat of the sun, he looked for a place to have lunch.

He thought about walking over to see the Alamo but decided to hold onto the memory of the time he and his son had made that trip together.

They had come for an American Idol contest tryout.

No luck on the tryout but it was a great father son trip.

He thought of him and knew he was now happily living with his partner in LA and working from home at what seemed to be a good job.

He spotted a sidewalk restaurant with tables in the shade of blue and white stripped canopies. Several blue and red barges carrying passengers along the river went slowly by and provided entertainment while he ate his spinach salad and nursed his iced tea.

He took another cab to John Friendly's used car lot where "Everyone was welcome and there was a car for everyone."

There he paid cash for a white Chevy Malibu.

At random, he selected a motel for the night. All he wanted was a clean, non-smoking room. It had been a long week with the robot fight team. A good night's sleep would be great.

The next morning, he drove to the East Jefferson bus station across the street from The University of Texas at Brownsville. The school's dark blue sign with large white lettering claimed the distinction of being Texas's south most college.

He wondered which college in Florida was claiming the to be the US's southmost college.

He drove around the back of the bus station to long term parking and walked back on a newly constructed brown brick inlayed sidewalk. He was becoming sensitized to the fact that brick sidewalks seemed to be the new fashion.

It was also clear that the station had undergone a total remodeling and sported a mixed brown, red and speckled black brick veneer.

He had seen what he thought were several entrances on the side where the University was located. He took what seemed to be a main side entrance.

He walked in onto a polished black and white terrazzo floor and walked up to a grey granite ticket counter that was just a little lower than chest high.

Looking around, he located a refreshment alcove at the far end and realized what he had initially identified as entrance doors were really bus loading doors.

The fare to Matamoros was a mere seven-fifty.

The dark complexioned, black-haired young lady with almost black eyes asked to see his passport. She provided him with a form that would serve as a tourist visa and asked him to fill it in.

Her perfect American English identified her as a young Latina that had grown up in the US. She was polite, and her smile gave her the beauty she seemed to know she had.

He finished using the counter to fill in his entry paperwork and then looked over to the refreshment stand wondering if he could get a cup of coffee with the change he had received when he paid for his tourist visa.

He took in the mix of people waiting for the bus as he walked slowly across the granite floor and the outline of Texas, and its major cities marked in inlayed brass.

The majority of people appeared to be Latinos. He was definitely in the minority and that concerned him. He hoped the group of young white, laughing and joking, backpacking travelers would be on his bus.

It turned out he needed to add another dollar to get a large cup of coffee. After the first taste, Ian wished it would have tasted as good as the look of the cup. Instead, it tasted more like the paper the cup was made of.

The wait for the bus was exactly a cup of coffee long and he knew he had taken his time to drink it.

Several other buses had come and gone, and it was clear that most of the Latinos were not going to go south across the border but were taking buses to other destinations. The loud group continued their boisterous ways and were clearly having a great time as they made their way to the bus he was taking.

He stood up and dropped his empty cup into the bin at the end of the row of seats. He was carrying a small backpack and nothing more. The suitcase he had left home with was in the trunk of his car in the long-term parking lot. The clothes he needed in Matamoros were to be delivered directly to the Holiday Inn.

The bus driver was loading the luggage, and the ticket agent was now checking to see that everyone had the proper paperwork ready and complete. She gave him a bright smile as he showed her his paperwork and waved him on board.

He sat in back and relaxed as he listened to the chatter of the group up front.

The first stop and check occurred on the US side before the bridge across the Rio Grande. The bus stopped, and two custom officers came on board.

One was a five-foot-five, body builder in appearance, pixie cut, steel grey haired no nonsense looking officer. Her biceps and forearms would have made any guy proud.

He had no doubt that if she were to lift her blouse there would be a ribbed six pack exposed.

She began to check the passports and visas in the front.

Her companion looked like a portly no-nonsense Curly, of the three stooges fame. His hair was cut short, probably done by himself or a cost-conscious wife. He presented a somewhat unfriendly, gloomy look.

He handed him his open passport and visa. He had looked at the name to reinforce his new persona.

The inspector asked him to open his backpack. It was clear to him that Curly had already made up his mind and was only doing a cursory check.

Only about five minutes passed before the bus was once again on its way.

The next stop was on the Mexican side of the border and the border patrol that came on board repeated the check.

It only took another thirty minutes to arrive at the main Matamoros bus station.

There he negotiated briefly with the driver of a white cab with 766 painted on the rear fenders.

The drive down highway 101 took another thirty minutes.

Two pinto palm trees loaded with their small yellow coconut like fruit, bracketed three flag poles.

One was flying the Mexican red, green, and white flag with the eagle and snake in the center, the US flag to its right and the state of Matamoros flag was on the left.

They seemed greeted his arrival to the off white six story tile roofed Holiday Inn.

The convention center, where the robot fight competition would take place was a tan, yellow colored square building the length and breadth of a football field featuring two pinto palms and a canopied entrance, stood to the right side of the hotel.

The cab dropped him off at the entry foyer.

A hotel porter opened the taxi door as he finished paying the cab driver.

"Hola, gracias," Ian said as he was led into the lobby.

He, dressed in a black short sleeved shirt, steel head grey khaki pants with black oxford shoes, followed the porter outfitted in a black suite, spit polished black shoes and white gloves through the two layers of self-opening sliding doors.

The transition from the dry hot air to the cool of the lobby was refreshing. The bustle of the lobby was quieted by the height of the lobby ceiling and the whir of the rotating overhead fans.

The porter led him to the reception desk where a young lady wearing a blue blouse awaited him.

Ian decided to practice his Spanish by asking about his hotel reservation.

"Hola, mi nombre es Trip Masters. Usted debe tener una reserva para *"Muerte de Norte"* combatir equipo," he said to the receptionist whose name tag identified her as Angela.

"Hola, señor Masters, tiene la habitación de la esquina en el quinto piso como usted pidió," she replied.

"I understand that I have the corner room five hundred one as requested. Thanks.

I would love to do this all in Spanish, but you are way past my ordering beer ability," he joked with her.

"No problem, I am fluent in English," Angela said with a Texas American accent as she flipped over to her second language.

"Por favor, Dígale al equipo que me llame cuando llegan," he asked Angela in Spanish. He hoped that he had asked about the arrival of the rest of the team.

"See you do know more Spanish. Sure, I will have them call you when they arrive," Angela replied with a smile that beamed a brilliant white.

He walked slowly across the lobby toward the two brushed stainless-steel elevators accented by a polished brass waste basket sitting between them and below a wooden framed pair of restaurant advertisements.

He got out on the fifth floor and proceeded to the corner room. He had splurged and rented one of the larger suites.

A four-person steel framed, glass topped table with four white padded chairs around it and a couch, chair and coffee table lay between the entrance door and the wet bar that had three tall white padded stools arranged in front of it.

The bedroom with a connecting bath was through a door to the left of the wet bar.

He closed the door behind him and put his small backpack on the floor and walked toward the wet bar and into the bedroom.

The marble in the bathroom immediately drew him in.

Pink and white marble covered the lower half of the walls and grey and white marble tile was used on the floor.

A wall-to-wall mirror spanned across the top of a marble counter with two pots of paper white flowers between two sinks.

A large Jacuzzi tub with a glass enclosed shower beside it filled the area across from the sinks.

The bathroom was almost as large as the bedroom behind him.

He turned and saw that his suitcase had been placed on a stand at the end of the bed.

He walked across to the suitcase and quickly unpacked. He wanted to get his shorts, gym shoes and tee shirt and do a quick workout in the hotel gym.

The bathroom was calling, and he wanted to enjoy the luxury of standing below the ceiling showerhead featured along with the normal showerhead. He hoped that the overhead shower would put out a heavy stream of water.

Later after returning from the workout, having enjoyed a long hot shower, he stood behind the wet bar counter.

He was surprised to find the two potted six-foot-tall palm trees bracketing the bar were real.

He was impressed to find the bar featured a small refrigerator with two Corona, two Modelo and two Negra Modelo.

There were also various kinds of soft drinks.

A separate wine cooler held a Riesling, a Cabernet Sauvignon, and a White Zinfandel.

His requests had been filled to the T.

He planned to entertain his team in his room.

He was very conscious of and feeling somewhat guilty about the situation he was putting the robot team in.

There was no danger to them, but he was definitely using them.

He had arranged for each member of the team to have separate rooms with a similar layout as his. The charge would go against his problem-solving expenses. He often imagined some secluded accountant trying to make sense of the expenses he submitted. None had ever been questioned and all had been paid.

The jangle of the bone-colored phone at the end of the bar brought Ian immediately back to the present. He had drifted into his problem analysis mode and had been leaning with his weight on his elbows on the bar.

He wondered how long he had been zoned out.

He picked up the phone and could hear the background noise of the hotel lobby.

"Trip," this is Dr. J. "We just arrived and are checking in. They say we have been upgraded at no cost. This is great."

"That is good to hear. Once you get settled, why don't you come up to room 501 and then we can plan where to go for dinner," he replied.

He already knew the restaurant where he wished to go.

He turned to look at the wine and beer glasses hanging behind him from the ceiling.

It would be interesting to listen to the reaction each of the team members would have about their rooms.

He called the concierge and asked if a cart of appetizers for six people could be arranged.

The concierge rattled off his suggestion of Pulled Pork Taquitos, Enchiladas, Black Bean and Sweet Corn Guacamole dip, Mini Chicken Chimichangas, and Quesadillas and a variety of corn chips.

He listened and then simply agreed.

The knock and the pattern clearly indicated Dr. J would be the person at the door. He walked over and opened it just as the rest of team could be heard down the hall getting off the elevator. Their chatter clearly indicated they were excited.

"I am in 502 across the hall in almost as nice a room as this but it does not have the bar. I can't believe we got such great rooms.

Is this your doing by any chance," Dr. J asked as he exaggerated his English accent and peered directly into Ian's eyes?

"Let's just say our benefactors were quite happy to upgrade the team," Ian replied as he waited with the door open for the rest of the team to arrive.

"This is already the best trip I have ever taken, and the tournament hasn't even begun," Samantha commented as she entered the room and stopped still, "Wow and I was just commenting that it couldn't get any better."

He watched as each team member in turn stopped to absorb the elegance of the room.

"What's your pleasure wine, beer or a soft drink," he inquired as the doorbell rang.

"Dr. J would you be so kind as to tend to the bar," he asked as he walked back to open the door.

He stood aside and watched as the server pushed in a large cart, opened the leaves of the cart, arranged the appetizers, and removed the lids.

"It just keeps getting better," Samantha reiterated as she stepped up to the appetizer cart and examined the offering.

He listened to the conversation and realized that eating out at the restaurant that he had planned to go in order to walk the area where he would carry out his problem-solving action was not going to happen on this evening.

The team attacked the appetizers with a gusto and a youthful energy he had forgotten.

He recalled several of the more memorable parties when he was a student at Stanford. He especially remembered the one where a beautiful dark-haired young lady with almost black eyes had escorted him to his dorm. He had pursued her until she had said yes to become his wife.

He suggested that rather than go out to eat, the better plan would be to go to the convention hall, check out the arrangements, unload *"Muerte de Norte"* and secure it in the team's assigned accommodation.

Then come back and eat in.

The resounding agreement confirmed Ian's read on the situation.

A half hour later the entire team walked down the hall to the elevator. Angela was still at the desk as Ian walked up and asked whether they needed a key to get into the building where the robot fighting tournament was taking place.

"Sí, el señor Trip, voy a tener el conserje organizar para alguien que te acompañe terminado," replied with a brilliant smile and a slight nod of her head.

He simply replied, "Gracias."

He led the team to the middle of the lobby, and they chatted about the coming tournament.

The outside of the hotel was now illuminated in the Holiday Inn green color. The lights at the entrance to the convention hall and the interior ones were all on. They were a day early and it appeared they were the only ones on location.

The facility was literally a football field in size but square. Most of the walls were folded back creating a huge open floor area. An eight-foot-wide half inch thick plate metal track led from what could have been taken as a glass enclosed boxing arena toward an area in the back of the facility. This last area had been divided and each team had a separate area to house their robot and their equipment.

The area opened to five truck dock doors.

He suggested the team bring *"Muerte de Norte"* in while he finished checking out the rest of the facility. He asked their escort to open up one of the bay doors before going on his own excursion.

He needed to be invisible in his coming and going. He located the surveillance cameras and looked for the blind spots. He repositioned a few cameras to create the blind spots he needed.

The invisible route out and back in was via the men's restroom. It had an entry from the tournament area and another from the hallway near a side exit door. There was one camera just above the backdoor of the bathroom.

He had a spray that did not blank out the camera but fogged it, so nothing was clear or distinguishable. This could be done from inside the bathroom by reaching out and spraying the camera covering lens.

The team was just finishing unloading and arranging all their equipment when he returned. Together they walked out to the front door where the hotel guide was waiting. The evening had cooled appreciably, and the air felt cool as they walked the short distance back to the hotel.

The younger members of the team were ready to party.

He suggested a quick break to allow each of them to go to their rooms. Afterwards, they could come to his room, and they would order dinner in and celebrate their arrival to the tournament.

The next two days were actually exciting. *"Muerte de Norte"* seemed unstoppable. It had won against each opponent and had only one more fight to win the tournament. The best part was that it had not yet used all of its arsenal, so it had a few surprises that had yet to be exposed.

The lasso technique had not been used.

"This is just fantastic, and I doubted my friend when he suggested we let you on our team," Dr. J commented.

Ian wondered who this friend was and how he was connected with his invisible supporters. He knew none of the details about his invisible support.

"Our final fight is scheduled tomorrow evening. We win it and we take home the trophy and the hundred grand prize," Marty commented.

"What time tomorrow evening," Ian asked.

He hoped it was not during the same time that the problem solution was to be delivered.

"Our match is set for nine pm. It was originally set for eight-thirty but the whole event has been running thirty minutes to an hour behind. Since they want to televise the final bout, they decided on the nine o'clock time frame," Samantha shared.

Ian doubted the time change was accidental. It appeared very coordinated with his plans.

During lunch the next day, he checked for the panel truck he expected to see in the parking lot.

The old dull tan van was parked at the end of the lot as he had requested. Its plain drab appearance and middle of the series selection was intentional. He was intent on making it hard for witnesses to remember it.

It was a relief to know that his support team, though invisible to him, was on the job and helping. He could now spend the day watching the robot fighters in the tournament eliminate each other.

The van had been modified to his specifications. An elevator to lower a flat box shaped robot to the ground had been installed. The elevator was remote controlled and worked off the same transmitter as the bomb robot.

The bomb robot was already on the elevator platform and would be lowered when commanded. The robot was a small flat square stainless-steel box. It was equipped with drive wheels and with a scissor jack lift. A high-grade explosive loaded in a cone shape depression would guide the explosion upward and hopefully keep it contained.

Everything was ready.

He had designed, built, and tested everything prior to having it shipped to where it now sat in the parking lot.

He smiled when he compared the design of the two robot units, that he was a part of designing. He had told the truth when he said that he built killer robots.

Activating the explosive charge was the only step remaining. He would do that once he reached the coffee shop.

"It's great to just be able to watch. *Muerte de Norte* has been so successful it got all the points to carry it to the finals," Dr. J. commented when he returned to where the team was sitting.

"I have a quick errand to run but I will be back for our final competition," he casually commented.

He walked into the restroom behind the refreshment stand. Two young men in jeans and matching green T shirts were commenting on the standings of various teams as they stood at their urinals. He walked casually past them and took the last stall near the back entrance and waited for them to leave.

He opened the rear door of the bathroom and sprayed the lens of the camera mounted on the wall above it.

He then stepped out into the hallway and walked out the back door.

He walked along the back wall of the center and then around to the right toward the front.

When he reached the front corner of the building, he stopped to look up at the position of the surveillance camera scanning the front lot and waited until it was pointed to the other end.

He then walked up to the van and casually got in. The tinted windows would conceal his presence. He took the time to check out his equipment and the robot. He also changed clothes and put on something more appropriate for the coffee house venue.

He started up the van and drove it slowly out of the parking lot. He drove up highway 101 until he reached the street where the coffee shop was located.

He was relieved to find one parking spot three cars behind where he knew the limo carrying the cartel leader would stop.

"Sometimes luck is as important as planning," Ian thought.

After parking the van as close to the curb as possible and once again verifying that the buildings on his left had no windows in them, he climbed into the back and activated the explosive charge.

A quick check let him know the elevator to lower the robot bomb to the street surface was working.

Everything he could do was now ready.

He opened the back doors of the van and stepped out. He could see no one as he took in the scene above the coffee shop. The lights and the black steel bars on the windows indicated they were occupied residences.

They should be OK.

The mariachi music coming from the coffee shop gave the area a cheerful sound and feel.

He straightened out his tan sports jacket, checked out the polish on his black boots and with a newspaper in hand walked across the street toward the shop.

A young waiter introduced himself as Enrico and asked where Ian would like to sit. His perfect English let Ian know that he had already been classified as one of the tourist gringos on vacation. He hoped this young man did not have too good of a memory.

He took a seat outside next to the wall to the right of the restaurant's large glass window. The inside of the coffee shop was already half full. The coffee shop would most likely have a good night.

"What can I get for you," Enrico asked as he cleared the extra place setting.

"Una taza de café y cuernos de azucar por favor," he asked for coffee and a roll in the best Spanish he could muster.

"Buena elección," Enrico replied with a large smile and walked into the shop to get the order.

Google Earth is like watching football at home on the big screen. You get a better view, and you get to see replays," Ian thought as he looked up and down the street as he tried to get oriented.

It was exactly what he expected.

He hoped things would turn out as expected.

He had his back to the wall, a cup of coffee, his sugar-coated crescent, and a newspaper in hand. He relaxed and tried to make sense of his Mexican newspaper.

Not too long afterwards a black Cadillac limo with darkened windows came slowly down the street and pulled into a spot two cars in front of his van that had been blocked by three orange cones.

He thought the fact that one of the leaders of the cartel actually went personally out to periodically talk to his victims spoke volumes about the need for direct feedback to his importance and power.

He had obtained the information on the routes of the bosses via a request to his unnamed supporters. They seemed to have the resources to find anyone anywhere.

Why was he needed?

"Perfect position," he thought as he looked from the van to the limo.

The black limo had not gone unnoticed.

The music was still playing inside, and he could hear the chatter from inside the coffee shop but the conversation at the outside tables seemed to have stopped.

Each person's dinner and coffee now seemed to take all of the attention. No one looked at the limo.

He pulled the small control module from his pocket and pushed the start button. He imagined he could hear the elevator in the van lowering the robot bomber. He put on what appeared to be his reading glasses and took a sip of his coffee. His glasses were polarized, and he was able to see the outline of the robot bomber as it slowly made its way under the car in front of the van, toward the limo.

He watched as a man dressed in a sleek black suite and spit polished black shoes stood up from one of the tables, took a sip of his coffee and then walked slowly across the street.

The driver of the limo came around and as he opened the door, the robot bomber raised up just in front of the gas tank and made solid contact with the bottom of the car. The explosion was aimed and would be contained in the back of the car.

"This will be an evening all of the clientele will remember," he thought as he waited for the businessman to exit the limo.

He took the last bite of his pastry and followed it with the last sip of his coffee.

He was glad he had paid when he had received the order. He put out a generous tip.

"Thank you, senor," a waitress walking by said as she picked it up.

"Asegúrese de compartir lo hará Enrico," he said in Spanish so she would think he knew Enrico, who had waited on him and that the tip was for him.

"Si of course senor."

He was becoming impatient when finally, the driver walked back around and opened the back door and the business owner stepped out and replied to something said from inside the car.

Ian was now at full attention. He hoped the business owner would get across the street before he had to activate the bomb.

Ian watched as the driver of the limo and the businessman seemed to be in a synchronized dance. Each were moving to their designated positions in slow time.

When he heard the slight rise in the engine noise and just as the car was about to move he pushed the fire button.

The blast hurled the business owner up onto the sidewalk. The limo rose three feet into the air and turned into a fireball. Glass came raining down on everyone out on the sidewalk and the four large glass panels on the front of the shop blew in on top of the patrons inside.

The smoke was overwhelming. The familiar taste of spent gun powder was on Ian's tongue and momentarily it took him back to his time behind the fifty-caliber machine gun in Vietnam.

He slowly picked himself up from the sidewalk where he had been hurled from his seat. He picked up his glasses and his newspaper and stumbled across the street to the van.

He was dazed.

The van had all of its windows blown out and as Ian started its engine, he could see that every window above the coffee shop had also been blown out. The car in front of the van had been blown back against the van and had all its windows blown out.

He wondered about the magnitude of the explosion.

He drove slowly away from the coffee shop. His mind raced as he tried to make sense of the blast's intensity. All he could think of, for the intensity of the explosion, was that the limo had been carrying a load of explosives in the trunk. His robot bomber had only enough explosives to penetrate the passenger area and eliminate anyone sitting in the backseat.

The driver would have survived the attack. Instead, everyone outside of the café was injured and the limo was a burning mass of twisted steel and contained two dead people.

The police cars with their alarms blaring approached rapidly and the area became a sea of flashing blue and red lights.

He drove slowly back to the hotel and parked the van in the location where he had found it. He cleared the shattered glass from his backpack and took out the clothes he had left the tournament in and put them on. He left everything else in the van.

He had to use a handheld piece of the rearview mirror to see the parking lot security camera. When the parking lot camera was pointed to the other end of the parking area, He exited the van and walked slowly along the back wall of the meeting hall. The long walk gave him time to recover. He was still in shock, and he figured he would have bruises all over his body.

He stepped into the bathroom. One person was just finishing washing their hands.

He remembered to wipe the entrance camera lens clean.

He stopped by the bathroom mirror and removed some black smudges from his cheek and put his hair in order.

He then returned to watch the remainder of the robot competition.

"You are just in time. The judges are insisting the entire team needs to be present for the final fight. We were getting worried," Dr. J said as he led Ian over to one of the judges to sign him in.

Once in the fight ring, *Muerte de Norte* rapidly decimated its opponent. It was the same as a knockout in the first round of a heavy weight boxing match. The issue of course was that there was not much fight time to broadcast.

"They want to do an interview with each of us," Samantha commented a few moments later.

"Sounds good," he said agreeably as he suggested they meet in his room to celebrate afterwards.

He edged his way toward the bar where he bought a beer and then blended into the crowd and faded away.

He was not about to get interviewed. He needed to stay anonymous.

As he crossed over to the hotel, he noticed the van was gone. He went up to his room and took a long hot shower. The blast had been strong enough that he would have a brick shaped bruise on his back and a bruise on his back side from having been bounced out of his chair. He knew he was lucky not to have been hit by flying glass.

A short time later he heard the team coming down the hallway toward his room. It was clear they were into celebrating their victory.

"You missed the interviews, but we sang your praises," Dr. J commented as he led the way through into the room.

"Let's get the celebration started at the bar and then we can call in our order," Ian replied.

It was early morning before the party broke up. Dr. J thanked him and walked out the door and crossed to his room.

He knew that the robot tournament would be an event he would long remember, and he would find some way to talk about it outside the context of his more lethal problem-solving actions.

The team met the next day at eleven to check out of the hotel. They still had to load "*Muerte de Norte*" into the truck and then begin their drive back to Illinois.

He accepted a ride with the team to the Laredo Airport.

The security checks on each side of the border went smoothly. One of the border agents who had watched the robot fight complemented the team on their victory.

At the airport everyone got out and gave him a hug and thanked him for helping them win the tournament.

"Well team have a great trip back. Maybe I will see you all next year," he said as he gave each of them a hug as they got back into the van.

He turned and walked into the airport ticket area and walked down its length and went down to the arrival area. He caught a cab to the bus station where his car was parked. He waited for the cab to leave and then walked to his car and drove away.

He was on his way to Laredo.

The local radio station reported the death of one of the key Gulf Cartel leaders. The blame was currently being pointed at rival cartels.

The news commentator spent a great deal of time speculating on the war between the rival gangs.

The news featured a witness that stated a large burly Mexican had driven away from the scene in a black van just as the police arrived.

He could not contain a chuckle. He had become a burly Mexican driving a black van. He thought about the difficulty of a blue eyed, white gringo to blend in.

"Blending in well," he continued his musing and hummed the tune to Yankee Doodle.

But the scene of the explosion kept playing his mind. He knew he was not OK. He had been alarmed at the power of the explosion and the people that had been hurt. He was experiencing something similar to PTSD.

He would need to keep a close watch on himself.

He heard the dark side of his mind laughing. He thought of Lesley and the kids, well his "adult" kids and got some semblance of control.

Normally he would have several weeks or months of time between problem-solving sessions.

Not this time.

The series of problem-solving events would be more like an ultra-marathon.

3 Laredo-Los Zeta Cartel

s Ian drove toward Laredo, he let his mind run through his research of the Los Zeta cartel. Their headquarters was in Nuevo Laredo across the border in Mexico.

The Los Zetas were originally comprised of a special forces group that had deserted the Mexican army to become the enforcers for the Gulf Cartel. After some leadership disagreements they had formed their own cartel and fought to control the area around Nuevo Laredo.

Ian had found their current leader Benito Solano-Solano interesting in that he had originally been on the good side but like Darth Vader in Star Wars he went over to the dark side.

Benito had joined the army straight from high school. He quickly rose through the ranks in the special forces unit and became a tough anti-cartel fighter. After losing many of his men because of repeated betrayals by his superiors he decided to change sides.

Benito was a young bright and very capable individual who had been successful in simultaneously fighting the Gulf Cartel, and the Mexican and US governments.

Mexico had a two-million-dollar reward, and the US had a five-million-dollar reward for information leading to his capture.

No one came forward for the reward. No one dared to do so. They knew that if they did, they would never live long enough to spend any of the reward.

Ian considered the Los Zetas to be one of the more dangerous targets because they operated with more discipline and paid more attention to security then most of the other cartels.

It was clear to Ian that both governments knew Benito's location. After all, he had found Benito's main operational compound just outside Nuevo Laredo three miles off Highway 2 using the internet and Google Earth. The two governments certainly had the resources to learn of Benito's whereabouts.

Ian realized that making contact with and taking any corrective action was going to be very difficult and extremely dangerous.

For this occasion, Ian was Martin Lindquist, a contributing reporter to the Boston Herald doing a report on the lives of Drug Cartel Bosses.

The official reason Ian was in Laredo was to try and get an interview with Benito. The "assignment" was to highlight Benito's humanitarian, family, and religious side. This was a different angle than most articles about Benito had focused on.

Benito was known to be a very effective, and thoroughly ruthless leader responsible for the deaths of many people. However, he was credited with donating the money to build the chapel in Santa Barbara in honor of Pope John Paul II.

Perhaps he thought good deeds might still get him into heaven.

Ironically, the church Benito gave money to was now under investigation for the potential use of illicit funds. This to Ian was ironic in that many people go to Rome and visit all the loot that has been accumulated from around the world and "given" to the Catholic Church. No one has thought of challenging their collection or the organization.

Ian stayed a few miles under the speed limit as he drove northeast on highway 83. The three-hour drive to Laredo would give him time to think through the plan and the various versions he had developed for his problem-solving session with the Los Zeta cartel.

Ian came into the Laredo area and took exit 3B and followed his GPS to the Goodwill store at the junction of San Dario Ave. and East Mann Rd. He was surprised at the upscale look of the store. The Goodwill business must be more lucrative than he was aware of.

The day had grown warm, and he was glad that he had dressed light. He parked the car and made sure he had all of his belongings out. He found the Goodwill store manager and followed her instructions on the car donation procedure.

In less than thirty minutes he had made his donation and was ready to walk to The Family Inn across the highway from the Goodwill.

He had chosen the location because of its proximity to the Goodwill store and was pleasantly surprised that it mirrored the pictures it posted on the internet. Ian gave it the name of "The Honest Family Inn."

The swimming pool in the center surrounded by palm trees made the place seem open and relaxing. Each of the first-floor units had a veranda and a four-person table. He was there for at least a night and looked forward to sitting out and reading.

Ian had his team book a room that featured a veranda. It had two queen beds and was quite well appointed. It was much better than he had been expecting.

After checking in Ian went to his room and put on his running shorts and jogging shoes. He put a pair of jeans and anything of value into his backpack and then went out for a jog.

The jog took him down San Dario Avenue alongside US 35. The constant tire hum was at first distracting but soon faded into white background noise. The heat of the day was just starting its late afternoon decline. It was as comfortable as it was going to get.

The cooking smells from the restaurants along the way went from Mexican to the smell of grilled steak coming from a place called the Sirloin Blockade. It all made Ian hungry.

The five-mile jog took Ian towards West Saunders Street where several used car lots offered a variety of transportation. He was aware of the dealer car lots that were much closer and just north of the Goodwill store, but he was looking for a place that would most likely be slower in processing its paperwork.

At a place called Bago's Auto, Ian stopped, took his jeans from his backpack, put them on and walked onto the lot. After a quick look around, he used cash to purchase a late model maroon SUV.

The interior of the SUV was in great shape, and it was evident that the car had gone through a thorough cleaning. The smell of the cleaning fluids was a little overpowering. Ian rolled down all the windows and drove out onto the street.

He drove with the windows open down San Bernardo Avenue to check out the Tornado Bus company and to see if they had a long-term parking area to leave the car. The lot behind the rather small station was available and would cost him fifty dollars for the time he would need to leave the car.

The bus ticket into Nuevo Laredo was only twelve dollars. The time choices for the ride across was either at the wee early hours of the morning, long before sunrise or the one single time at four-thirty in the afternoon. He quickly made the decision to go across the following afternoon.

Ian had the rest of the evening and the next day. He would have preferred to be in Nuevo Laredo earlier, but he had no clue what he would do there at three in the morning. Who had decided on such a time for a bus route?

It was time to go to dinner and then get a good night's sleep. Maybe the ache in his buttocks, caused by being blown out of his chair during the explosion in Matamoros, would feel better after another day of rest. He laughed to himself about having a real pain in the butt.

He chose to have dinner at the Compos Bar and Grill, one of the better rated nearby restaurants. Ian was early and there was at least another hour of daylight, so he considered the outdoor seating, but the view consisted of the shopping strip's parking area or the side of a shopping store across the street.

Inside was a little dark but overall was an acceptable atmosphere. Every item on the menu attracted him. He chose a Lamb and Scallop appetizer, an Ahi Tuna Salad, and a bottle of Pellegrino.

He recalled similar diners where he ate whatever his sons and friends wanted and that was prepared by an eager mother. He always had his glass of Pellegrino.

While he waited on the food, Ian went to the web site of his new identity to continue his transition from Trip Masters, design engineer to being Martin Linquest reporter for the Boston Herald. It's always nice to know your bosses name and what you have been writing for the last twenty years Ian thought to himself as he sat and reviewed his website appropriately named Martin's View.

His support team had created a website that went back multiple years and had some very interesting articles. He smiled as he became sensitized to what a great writer he was.

The next morning Ian stayed and had breakfast at the hotel. The splashing sounds from the water fall and the kids playing on the slides and swings opposite of the swimming pool relaxed him. He sat at the blue green tiled gazebo counter and had a simple breakfast of bacon and eggs, a pancake, and a cup of coffee.

He watched the face of the waitress as she put his over easy eggs on top of the pancake. He asked for extra syrup. After pouring all the syrup on the pancakes and putting pads of butter between them, he broke the yellow of the eggs and began eating the syrup-soaked pancake with a piece of the egg.

After breakfast Ian arranged to check out late in the afternoon and then retreated to the veranda in front of his room to think about his coming problem-solving engagement and to continue his review of Martin Linquest's web site. His very interesting website!

Martin Linquest had been born in Ian's imagination. Building a believable web presence and getting it appropriately posted required the expertise of his invisible support team. He had asked for their support and was given the message to generate the report article outlines and interviews.

Ian figured he should have become a fiction writer. It had taken him longer to generate the years of history present on the web site than the work he had done in getting ready for the robot fight team. He had sent the material into his support group, and they had created and populated the web site. He was sure they could do anything they wanted and put anytime stamp they wanted on any material. The internet was fantasy land to Ian.

Anything and everything was possible.

Martin Linquest was on Facebook, had his own heavily followed blog and had articles in many of the national journals.

Ian remained on the veranda with a slight breeze blowing between the buildings that kept the veranda at a warm but pleasantly comfortable level. The laughter of three six-to-eight-year-old kids in the pool created a peaceful atmosphere.

He skipped lunch and joined the kids in the pool.

Finally, at three Ian checked out and drove to the bus station.

Ian parked the SUV snug to the back wall of the bus station. He paused to look at the orange, red and blue strips painted horizontally on the wall of the station before grabbing his backpack from the right front seat.

His one suitcase was in the back.

Looking around the area he wondered whether the car would remain here for the week. There was little he could do about it if it got stolen.

He got out and walked around to the front of the station.

Three blue bus seats graced the front of the bus station office. They were occupied by an older white-haired man, what appeared to be his wife and a teenager probably fifteen or sixteen.

Ian stood at the corner of the building behind a silver pickup truck. It appeared the three were all waiting for the same bus.

When the bus arrived, it was clear there had been several other stops and some of the passengers looked as if they had been riding for a long time.

Ian gave the driver his ticket and was reminded he needed a valid passport, or a tourist permit as he boarded.

The passenger pick-up took less than five minutes and the bus pulled away five minutes early.

Ian noted as they crossed into Mexico, that the Rio Grande was not so grand, and it had little water in it.

The Mexican border guards boarded the bus and checked everyone's passports and then the bus proceeded.

The air blowing from the ceiling vents made conversation difficult and most of the passengers were quietly looking out the windows.

At the bus station, Ian was about to get into a cab when he spotted a van with the name Fiesta Crowne Plaza with the distinctive yellow circle with three golden horizontal squiggle lines.

The older couple and the teenager were all pulling their suitcases toward it.

Ian walked over and asked if there was room for one more.

The ride took less than fifteen minutes. Ian was taken by the fact that the teenager played some game on his i-pad and the older couple were completely silent. The family connection did not exist.

Ian rode in silence himself but found it hard not to start a conversation. Had he been on a different mission he would have done so but at the moment he wanted to remain as unnoticed as possible.

The hotel catered to the North American tourist. Its distinctive emblem was at the top of a twelve-story brick column enclosed stairs that went up the side of the building.

The older couple and the teenager seemed to rush away from the van as Ian took his time, thanked the driver, and gave him a tip.

The four threes' numbers to the right and just above the height of the double sliding door entrance caught Ian's eye. This was an easy address to remember.

The door opened to an expansive brightly lit lobby.

A receptionist, dressed in a dark blue business dress and matching jacket over a light blue blouse with thin vertical stripes and a gold necklace with a heart strategically hanging in the v above the top of the blouse button, stood below a red brass enclosed oval with the three horizontal stretched triple S symbol above foot high lettering boldly announcing the hotel's name in giant bold letters and in smaller letters below it gave the location, Nuevo Laredo.

The grey and black granite counter Ian was walking toward stretched in the same shape across the entire back of the lobby. The front of the counter had lights shining down illuminating bone-colored panels with white swirls.

Five clocks on the wall to the receptionist's left provided the times for Laredo, Los Angeles, Chicago, New York, and London. The entire check-in area was brightly lit by recessed lights beaming down from ten feet above.

Ian walked up to where the receptionist was standing and was greeted by a smile that lit up her face and flashed her bright white teeth. Her hair hanging down each side to almost to her waist provided the perfect frame for her pleasant sisterly face.

Ian gave her his new name, Martin Lindquist, and handed her his passport.

"Yes, Senor Linquist we have been expecting you. We have the style of room you asked for with a king-size bed, a work desk, a separate table, and a nice chair to sit in. I hope you like it," she said as she found his reservation and checked him in.

Ian took the elevator to the seventh floor and went to his room where he unpacked his suitcase, hung up his clothes and put his personal computer into the safe. He put out the various reports and memos that solidified Martin Linquest as a real person.

He expected that some time on this trip his room would be searched.

Ian returned to the almost empty lobby. He took a walk around and got a better feel for the hotel, its bar, restaurant and sitting area. The gym had a good mix of equipment and four treadmills. He would probably not have time for the swimming pool but its presentation of reclining lounge chairs below small palm trees all the way around the pool was sure to capture the attention of everyone.

Ian returned to the lobby and approached the concierge and asked about the night spots and if by any chance he could arrange to have a driver that would stay with him as he tried each place out.

Ian wanted to hit as many places as possible on his first night. He planned to make the round several times in hopes of making contact with the Los Zeta Cartel.

"Si, yes, my cousin would love such an opportunity. Can you wait about fifteen minutes for him to get here," the concierge whose name tag identified him as Diego replied?

"Diego, is he available for the week," Ian continued his inquiry?

A few minutes later, Ian looked at a person entering the lobby that he presumed was the cousin. He was dressed in a plain light blue T shirt, blue jeans, and light blue slip-on tennis shoes. His black hair, dark brown eyes and open smile immediately made him seem a good choice. Ian watched as he walked over and talked to Diego.

Ian stood up as the two approached him.

"Senor Linquest, I am Raul. I would be pleased to be your driver this week. How many hours each day do you want me to be available," Raul inquired.

His direct manner, inquiry and seeming confidence in his carriage and his voice pleased Ian.

Ian decided on the spot that he would hire Raul. Now it was just a matter of getting through the bargaining.

Ian would pay whatever it took but he always bargained so the recipient of the money would feel he had gotten a good deal.

"I am not sure. Why don't we agree on ten hours a day whether I need you or not? Some days it may be less and maybe there will be a time when it is more. What will it cost for such an arrangement," Ian inquired?

Ian watched as Raul thought about the situation and was pleased when he came to a quick decision.

"Ok Senor Linquest, fifty dollars each day including today, and you pay for the gas," Raul put forward his offer.

Ian knew he could bargain the price down significantly but chose instead to add some requirements that he knew would be easily accepted.

"Fifty dollars each day but you must call me Martin, take me to eat at the good Mexican restaurants you would want to go to, and show me all the night spots in Nuevo Laredo. You cannot drink alcohol during this week, not even a beer," Ian replied.

Ian was serious about the drinking. He did not want to end up in an accident as the two of them went from bar to bar.

"Senor, I mean Martin, you drive a very hard bargain," Raul replied as he feigned pain by putting his hands on his chest.

Ian could tell from the response and the look Raul gave to his cousin that it was good for him.

OK, I will pay you half now and when I make contact with Benito Salano-Salano you get the other half, but then your employment is over, and you will not contact me after that contact is made.

Both Raul and Diego's eyes went wide, and they inhaled in unison and both uttered,

"Jesús, Oh mi dios, eres loco," Diego uttered.

"Yes, I suppose I am crazy. I am here to see if I can get an interview with him for the Boston Herald about his personal life and aspirations.

"Martin, perhaps you should pay all up front, so I do not have to look in your wallet after they kill you," Raul joked.

Ian understood both the joke and the concern about getting paid.

"OK, I will give you three hundred now, an extra fifty dollars for gas and I will put another two hundred in an envelope with your name on it in the office safe. You can pick it up on Friday, but you must promise to stay out of my wallet," Ian finished with a joke.

Ian opened his black leather two chamber wallet with a hidden third pocket covered by the back flap. He counted out fifteen twenties and handed it over to Raul. He then counted out another fifty. Please count it and sign this receipt. I want the Herald to reimburse me later. Ian instructed.

He watched as Raul slowly counted and then signed the receipt.

Ian accepted the receipt and then walked across the lobby to the check-in desk and asked for an envelope. He put the other two hundred and a generous tip into the envelope and asked the receptionist to put this in the safe until Friday when a Raul Lopez would pick it up.

"Please wait here and I will bring the car to the hotel entrance," Raul said as he hurried toward the hallway leading to the back of the hotel.

The car sparkled in the lights shining down from the light pole. As Raul opened the front passenger door for Ian the cool interior air presented the faint smell of lavender. The interior was spotless. It was hard to tell the year of the car and it did not matter. It was in pristine condition.

Ian's appraisal of Raul went up dramatically.

Ian asked Raul if he had dinner yet. Raul had not, so Ian suggested that they go to the best Mexican restaurant Raul could think of but one that did not cater to the Gringos.

The night lights of Nuevo Laredo and what Ian considered an erratic driving style typical of his many experiences as a passenger in Mexico made the drive to Raul's favorite place stimulating.

The small square cement block building painted in a light yellow with four plain glass windows and a glass front door all trimmed in white, was located on the corner of two busy streets. The building wore a yellow panel around the roof with one forest green and one dark red stripe and proudly declared *"Polo Frito Fiesta"* with the words alternating red, green, red in color and on the front of the building the sign declared it as the best chicken in the city.

Ian followed Raul in and listened as he was greeted by the plump but very friendly woman behind the counter.

Ian took in the four well-worn but solid wooden tables along the front. The cooking was done in a grill behind the building and the mouth-watering aroma seemed to tempt the appetite each time the door was opened.

Ian followed Raul to the only available table at the end of the row.

A young version of the person behind the counter came to take their orders. Her broad white toothed smile, the swing of her hips and her greeting made it clear to Ian she was flirting with Raul. Raul looked at Ian, raised his left eyebrow, and smiled.

Ian sat back and enjoyed watching the interplay of the two young people. It was refreshing to see this dance take place in all corners of the world.

He agreed with Raul to try each style of the chicken and to sample the chicken salad. Raul ordered a soft drink and Ian asked for a bottle of tonic water.

The chicken was brought to the table on a plate lined with waxed paper with the chicken on top. Two small round plastic tubs offered two different white sauces to dip the chicken into. Ian liked the plain salt and pepper seasoned chicken the best. The hot wings were also very good, and the coated or breaded chicken was delicious.

Raul asked which he liked best. Ian decide that he liked them all and agreed that it was some of the best chicken he had eaten. He made the point that only his wife, Lesley, prepared a better chicken.

Raul turned out to be a good guide. He seemed to know all the night spot locations and the reputation each carried. Though each had a different atmosphere, all night spots had the same feel of people seeking some sort of relief from daily life, the goal of some connection with other people and the hope of finding one's purpose in life.

The discussion with the bar tenders and their common alarmed reactions when he inquired about meeting Benito Salano-Salano was almost a duplicate of Raul's reaction to the fact that he must be crazy.

However, in each case Ian left his Boston Herald business card with his cell number and his current hotel written on the back.

After visiting three-night spots, and leaving a business card at the bar, Ian decided it was enough for one night. He arranged to have lunch with Raul on the following day and then they would continue the visits to the bars.

The next morning Ian arose late, got up, went to the gym for a quick workout, came back to the room, took a quick shower and was in the lobby a few minutes before twelve.

Diego greeted him and asked how the previous evening had gone and if Raul was doing a good job.

"Raul won the day at the beginning by taking me to eat some of the best chicken I have ever eaten," Ian replied.

"Si I am sure he took you to Polo Frito Fiesta. Not only is the chicken very good but a very good-looking chicken that he likes works there for her mother," Diego said with a small laugh.

Raul's green car stopped at the front doors. The car was shiny and spotless. Raul must have cleaned it during the morning.

Ian said goodbye to Diego and walked out just as Raul pulled up to the hotel.

Raul suggested they take lunch at the El Ranchero restaurant he identified as an upscale place.

The exterior of the stucco building featured five arches topped by a second story with matching glass doors coming out to two small terraces that bracketed the outside seating area on the second floor.

The brown, red color of the arches and the black painted railing of the terraces and top deck topped with what appeared to be a giant plate with the years 1972-1993 arched over them impressed Ian.

Ian followed Raul in through the center arch leading to the entrance.

The interior was an onslaught of bright green, yellow, red, and blue colored mural scenes of Mexican life and key moments in history stretching around the seating area.

The tables were covered with light lime green table clothes. A second smaller tablecloth on top had dark green strips on an orange background.

The plain white panel ceiling was the only feature that seemed out of place.

The restaurant had a spacious setting with at least thirty tables.

Ian and Raul followed the receptionist to one of the tables roughly in the center of the room.

Ian decided that all Mexican restaurants carried the great smells of the foods they served. Steaks and beef dishes seemed to be popular at the El Ranchero. The sound of sizzling meat being carried out to the various tables immediately told Ian that the Fajitas must be good. He looked around several tables to get a better feel for the menu.

The sizzling Fajitas in their cast iron frying pans carried out on their wooden platters proved to be Ian's choice.

Raul and Ian were both drinking Pellegrino. The room was about three quarters full, but the high ceiling and the sound absorbing ceiling panels made quiet conversation possible.

A good choice of ceiling, Ian thought as he recalled his initial evaluation.

Ian ask Raul about his personal status. It turned out Raul was trying to work himself through school and was currently enrolled at the Instituto Tecnologico de Nuevo Laredo in their engineering program.

He had applied to several Universities in the US but had not been accepted at any of them. He was still trying to get into some US college in hopes of getting a path out of Nuevo Laredo.

Ian made a mental note to make a call to Dr. J and see if he could get Raul admitted on a scholastic scholarship. He was sure a reasonable gift to the engineering robot program would help in getting Raul admitted.

The next part of the conversation took Ian by surprise. Raul looked around as if there might be someone listening and then commented that one of his buddies knew where Ian could make contact with the cartel.

The food arrived, and Raul stopped talking until the waitress left.

"I will tell you more later in the car," Raul continued.

Ian was curious, but he preferred having the remainder of this conversation in the car as well. He initiated a conversation about Raul's family and his goals for the future.

The night visits to the various night clubs were a duplicate of the evening before. Ian had done his field work and visited most of the local pubs and coffee houses and asked questions about Benito. He was hoping to get noticed by the cartel and get invited to talk to the boss himself.

As the evening ended, Raul let him know that they had covered the majority of the entertainment spots.

Raul then shared the location of a restaurant where the cartel supposedly held many of their meetings.

It was only nine in the evening, but Ian decided to call it a day and asked Raul to give him a ride to that restaurant in the morning.

Ian walked into the quiet almost empty hotel lobby. Diego was still on duty and gave a furtive wave for him to come over.

"Senor Linquest, be careful, they have been in inquiring about you, and I think they went to your room. They left only a short time ago," Diego said in a hushed tone.

"Gracias Diego, it was good of you to let me know," Ian replied.

It was good to know that his inquiries had been heard.

Ian felt that giving Diego money for the information he had shared would be taken the wrong way, so he walked over to the check in desk and asked for an envelope into which he put two hundreds and put Diego's name on in with instructions to give it to him on the coming Friday.

Ian went to his room. Everything was as he had left it. The only way he knew that his room had been searched was the broken hair he had taped to the bedroom door.

He smiled. It seemed he had the attention of the cartel.

Sleep came easily, and he had a good night.

4 Laredo-Connection

*T*he next morning as he walked through the lobby, he noticed a different concierge was on duty. He wondered if Diego had purposely taken the day off.

Raul was exactly on time and arrived as Ian walked out of the lobby doors.

The early morning sky had that sleepy grey look, and the air had a moist feel. Ian knew that the cool of the morning would quickly dissipate and be replaced by the still hot air that had been yesterday afternoon.

"Buenos días Raúl, ¿cómo fue tu noche," Ian asked as he got into the front passenger seat.

"Thank you for asking. I had a great evening and even got my homework done," Raul replied.

The restaurant was only two minutes from the hotel. A tall imposing statue of someone named Juarez stood at the center of a traffic circle immediately in front of the restaurant that featured a windmill in what appeared to Ian to be a competition of height with the statue out in the circle.

Ian had Raul drop him off by the statue of Juarez and told him that he would call by noon if he needed transportation. He did not want Raul to be anywhere near the restaurant unless he was called back.

The smell of bacon and of fried beans in the restaurant immediately reminded Ian that he had skipped dinner the evening before. The big decision was whether to have two eggs with a waffle or a more traditional Mexican breakfast meal.

After a brief look at the menu and examining the orders of the people around him, Ian decided on the Barbacoa breakfast of enchiladas, coffee with cream and a bottle of water.

Ian was just finishing putting cream into his coffee and stirring it absent mindedly when a premonition made him look up as the door to the restaurant opened. Ian immediately recognized the person coming through the door as the Zeta leader, known as Z-20 and nicknamed Pepino, *the hot one.* The birth name his mother had given him was Jorge.

The utter silence in the room screamed its warning as all the customers focused on their food or drink and averted their eyes away from where Z-20 was going.

A cold shiver went up Ian's back. There was no gun present, but Ian was at full alert and ready for anything. This was a guy that caused local journalists to quake in fear and caused some to disappear.

He watched as a second person stood by the door and Z-20 walked slowly and directly toward him.

"Good morning, Senor Linquest. I understand you would like to interview me. I am Benito Salano-Salano. What questions do you have for me," he said as he sat down?

"Good Morning, Senor Pepino. May I offer you a cup of coffee? I have just ordered breakfast. You are welcome to join me," Ian replied as he looked steadily back at Z-20 and pushed an empty cup toward him and lifted the coffee pot to pour a cup.

"An interview with you would be very interesting and put icing on the cake for my readers. I am trying to get a different perspective about the daily lives of the cartel leaders. My readers would love to hear about your daily family life and interactions. The drug statistics get boring after a while."

"So, you have at least done some homework on who we are. You know that I am the enforcer," Z-20 replied as he leaned toward Ian across the table trying to intimidate him with his persona.

His gaze was an effective way to cool any sort of passion and to sow fear into most people.

"Yes, I am aware of your reputation, and I hope to stay on your good side. I know the basics of the drug business. I am not interested in any of that."

I am interested in your personal life outside of your business. Do you go to church? Do you have a wife, or a girl friend? Do you play poker on Saturday night? My readers want to know the human side of the cartel bosses. These are the type questions my interview will focus on," was Ian's quiet reply.

Z-20 sat looking at Ian for several minutes apparently thinking. Ian hoped he was thinking good thoughts. Ian looked back steadily and waited.

"Don't show the enforcer any sign of fear," was the phrase that went through Ian's mind and there was no fear on his part.

Ian knew that if the enforcer made a move against him at this range, the enforcer would be dead before he could get his hands-on Ian or put a gun into use. The only worry Ian had was in how many support persons Z-20 had with him.

"Ok, tomorrow afternoon a car will pick you up at your hotel. You will be taken to meet with Benito. He said if you were legitimate, he would see you. I will be there as well. Do not bring any computer, phone, or recorder. You will work with pencil and paper only. Is that agreeable," Z-20 inquired?

It was clear to Ian he knew which hotel. His people were probably the ones that had searched his room and gone through his things. Ian hoped they had been thorough. He had worked hard to have the right information to convince them of his liberal leaning and his past reporting.

They could even go on his website and read past articles and comments. Ian was sure they had. Martin Linquest had a long history on the web.

"Pencil and paper, it is. I will be waiting. What time," Ian replied?

"Afternoon. Be patient, relax with a drink at the bar. Someone will come in and show you this coin," he said showing Ian a coin with Sapano emblazoned on both sides.

He stood up, gave Ian a hard stare that Ian returned evenly, Z-20 then turned and walked briskly away.

Ian looked around to see if anyone had taken notice of the event.

"Of course, we noticed," everyone screamed in their total silence and unwillingness to look toward his table.

His breakfast appeared as soon as the restaurant door closed.

The non-reaction at the coffee house was more chilling than the effect Z-20 had on Ian. People were so frightened they literally refused to acknowledge the existence of the person. In the process it seemed that Ian had become invisible as well.

The appealing smell of the pork enchiladas pulled Ian back and his gaze returned to his table. He topped off his coffee and slowly poured in some cream from the small white ceramic pitcher. The clink of his teaspoon against the side of the cup seemed to echo across the now silent dining area.

It was clear to Ian that the place would not return to normal until he left the premise. To them, he had become a potentially virulent germ ready to infect anyone who might get too near.

He purposefully took his time and enjoyed his meal before calling for the check.

Ian walked across the parking lot and then dashed across the traffic circle and sat down on the wall that created a pool at the base of the statue.

He called Raul, to let him know that contact had been made, thanked him for his services and told him to pick up the remainder of his money at the hotel desk.

Ian then sat and thought through the scenarios for his upcoming interaction with Benito.

Once he had thought through the variations Ian walked the six blocks back to the hotel. It was almost exactly noon as he walked across the lobby to the desk.

Ian instructed the desk clerk to allow Raul to pick up his envelope whenever he came in and he wanted to make sure Diego was given his envelope the next time he came in for work.

The attitude of the desk clerk had changed. She found it hard to talk directly to Ian. He was sure this was the result of the cartel's visit. She knew that he was being watched by the cartel and not sure she wanted to be associated with him or be too friendly to him.

Ian went up the elevator and put the key card up to the lock and heard the click as the lock activated. He was sure the guys who had come into the room had come in exactly the same way. Most probably with a card given to them by the young clerk who could not look him in the eyes.

Contact had been made and now it was time to relax.

Relaxing turned into a night long sleep. Ian could not recall getting into bed and was surprised when he woke up and looked at the door to see a chair wedged against the inside handle of the door.

He looked at the clock on the bedside table and let out a small groan. It was just past seven in the morning. He was terrible at waiting and he had until sometime in the afternoon before he was to be picked up.

On his way to breakfast he saw that Diego was at the concierge's position and gave him a slight nod as he walked past. Diego winked back but otherwise did not acknowledge him.

It was clear that Ian was now dangerous to be around. Ian understood and went on to the restaurant for a breakfast of two pancakes with butter and syrup, two over easy eggs with bacon or sausage and a cup of coffee with cream.

By late afternoon, Ian had worked out in the gym, sat in the ninety-two-degree hot tub where he spent some time determining that 35 degrees Celsius was approximately 95 degrees Fahrenheit.

Breakfast had lasted long enough, and it had been large enough that Ian again chose to skip lunch and he was now sitting at the lounge bar with a large bottle of Pellegrino and a glass as he waited for someone to walk up to him and show him the two-sided Sapano-Sapano coin.

Ian thought through various scenarios once again and concluded that success meant he would cross back across into the US no matter the outcome of the solution attempt. There was no failure scenario, only a success scenario. This realization made the next sip seem exceedingly sweet and fresh.

For the first time that day Ian actually relaxed, and he decided to order a gin and tonic with a twist of lime, without the gin.

Success or failure, Ian would cross the border and move on to the next cartel. There would be no, second chance or second attempt.

Three tonic waters later, a rather gentle, mild looking young man with slicked back black hair, a quiet voice put a Sapano coin on bar and then a moment later flipped it over to show Ian the Sapano on the other side. His mild voice softly said, "follow me."

Ian looked up from his tonic and knew he was looking at the deadliest person he had met so far on this trip. The black eyes were blank. This was a killer that had no emotions. A shiver ran down Ian's back. This was not someone Ian would trust. He would never allow him to be behind him.

Ian's immediate reaction was to observe the young man's movement and mannerisms. Ian decided that the weapon of choice for this young man would be a knife or straight razor used like a butterfly knife.

A shiver again ran down Ian's back. It was not the lion's den that he was going into but the devil's torture chamber.

The windows of the car were darkly tinted, and Ian could barely make out to the surroundings.

"Relax senor, it will be about thirty minutes before we get to our destination," the young man said quietly from the front seat.

Ian noted that they were indeed going down what he thought was highway two toward the compound he had located during his research.

They turned off the highway onto a hard dry dirt road.

The road back to the compound was several miles long and went through some rough terrain with sharp drop offs into deep dry ravines.

This part of the trip was slow going. It was a scenic dry desert with red flowers blooming from the ends of their paddle-like branches. The crevasses were greener than the surrounding landscape. The slow approach helped Ian get oriented to the many twists and turns. He was attentive and absorbing the surroundings as fully as possible.

"This country has a raw beauty all its own," he said in a friendly kind of way.

"Si," was the driver's brief reply.

The limo approached a walled compound and came to a stop to wait as three-inch-thick, ten-foot-high wooden gates rolled open to one half to each side. Once the gates retracted the car left the gravel road and entered a large smooth black cobble stone paved center courtyard.

A circular garden in the center with a flowering cactus was the main theme. The interior gardens were immaculate and manicured. Thick green grass framed the circular driveway.

The front door was probably forty inches across and eight feet high and the person standing in front of it obscured most of it.

Once the car came to a stop the hulk stepped forward and opened the back door for Ian.

His high voice did not match his build and Ian almost let out a chuckle.

"Slap yourself on the back of your head and behave. You don't want to make this guy mad," Ian thought to himself.

"I will need to pat you down," was the giant's only comment.

He held the same type of metal detector used at the airport security check points.

Ian dutifully spread his legs and held out his arms. The pad and pencil were in his left hand and nothing in his open right hand.

"Follow me," was all that was uttered by my young escort when the pat down was complete.

Again, Ian was comforted to be following versus having him behind. They entered a large room that seemed to be a library and gathering area. A billiard table was the central focus and shelves of books and large comfortable-looking leather chairs with small tables next to them went around the wall.

It was definitely a male oriented setting.

Ian conjectured that Benito was single and normally did not have women out for any length of time. He had seen no indication of a woman's touch.

"Please wait here," was the brief instruction.

Ian chose a chair facing the entrance to the room and his back to the wall. Ian flashed back to L.A. and another similar room. Three very bad people had died in that room. He hoped to be as successful here as he had been then.

This situation was much riskier than the previous one. Ian felt like he was being watched and was certain that he was.

The bar to the right of the entrance was well stocked and displayed some fine whiskeys and beers on tap. A bottle of Courvoisier Cognac and two classes were on the bar top.

It seemed to be prepared for Salano-Salano and him.

Ian always thought it interesting that it was the disgruntled Dutch settlers who found it difficult to preserve the French wine and through a series of distillations invented "Brandy" which comes from "brandewijin" meaning burnt wine.

Many of these Dutch settlers were smugglers too. Of course, that was a different time, and the goods were of a different nature.

Ian's musing came to an end as Benito walked into the room. He was as handsome as his pictures. In person he seemed like any other friendly good looking, black haired, black eyed, youngish looking handsome Mexican man.

Benito approached and introduced himself. Ian took note that he did not extend his hand in greeting.

It was clear to Ian that Benito was going to be polite, but not friendly.

"I am Benito. I understand you have been asking about me and would like to interview me," he said politely as Ian, and he looked steadily at each other.

"I am Martin Samuel Linquest," Ian said using all three names.

He knew in Mexico the names sometime would take on a meaning of their own.

"Yes, I am interested in doing an article on the personal side of your life. Your business side is well documented and has been written about exhaustively. However, my article will delve into who is Benito Salano-Salano, the person who built the church, who has donated substantial money to various charities.

Perhaps there are other stories of other good deeds that may not be known to the general public," Ian continued his introduction in a quiet even reply.

Ian was watching Benito's reaction closely. No one had entered the room with him. This was a bad sign for Ian because it meant they were being remotely monitored. For sure, there would be no aggressive action taken on Ian's part in this room.

"What can I offer you to drink," Benito asked as he indicated the bar.

"I would prefer either plain tonic or soda water, no ice," was Ian's reply.

Ian seldom drank hard liquor and, on this occasion, even a beer would not do.

A person came in through the door and went behind the bar. He opened a can of Canada Dry tonic and poured a shot of the Courvoisier.

It was clear they might be the only ones in the room, but they were not alone. Ian figured the help was probably in an adjacent room. It most likely opened directly into this one via one of the bookshelf walls. They were on an open stage. Their audience was just out of sight.

The pen may be mightier than the sword but here Ian stood with only a pencil. It was a weapon he had wielded many times in a very deadly fashion but in this case, it was hardly adequate.

Ian decided to focus on the interview.

"How do we do this interview," Benito asked.

"Well, I think perhaps the easiest way would be for you to describe all the good deeds you have done. Let them be stories from early on until now. I will listen and take notes. Later I will write a story from what I have heard and the notes I take," Ian replied.

"Will I be able to look at your notes," he asked?

"Yes, you can look at my notes before I leave, and I will send you the copy I turn in. I will also make sure you will get a copy of the paper that it is published in. Who knows, it may actually be picked up globally and you will be famous," Ian replied.

Apparently, I am already famous. I am just not well known as a good person he replied as he took a sip of the brandy.

Benito went back to his early days. His early school days were recalled fondly, and he recounted the wonderful time he had. He had been popular with the girls but had never met the right one.

"Not finding the right partner has been the continued disappointment in my life," Benito commented.

"In my early life, my family was not rich and did not have the money to send me to the University. I enlisted in the Army and qualified for the special force's unit. This was a good fit for me," Benito continued.

"I was very successful and rose to commander in a short period of time. Soon it became apparent to me that the sacrifices my troops were making in fighting the cartels was not supported by the corruption in the Army's top leadership."

"It was during a raid on the Gulf Cartel that it became clear to me that I could no longer sacrifice the men under my command and watch these senior army leaders take in their money with the blood of my men on it."

"It's like in the Star war movie, I went to the dark side. Here I have better control of my environment. My family now has the money to live well. I have been able to give money to the charities I believe do good and to the Church."

"Why don't we continue this interview over dinner," Benito abruptly suggested.

"Thank you, that would be great," Ian responded. Having skipped lunch, he was feeling hungry.

"Follow me."

Ian dutifully took his pad and pencil and followed Benito out the door, down the hallway to a large room with a long table large enough to seat twenty. Two places were set across from each other on one end.

Once again this was evidence to Ian that he was surrounded by an invisible but attentive group of people all working for Benito.

"Not in this house, perhaps not this time," flashed through Ian's mind.

The light conversation continued. Benito periodically would fill in another story.

Ian reflected on the great interview he was getting.

And the dinner was a delicious Argentine steak cooked rare and served with rice and Mexican beans. A separate mixed salad rounded out the dinner.

Ian relaxed, took notes, and enjoyed the meal. Nothing was going to happen as long as they were in this fortress of a compound.

Ian looked at this to be a failed problem-solving session. That was OK since he was starting to like this ruthless drug lord.

It was a delicious meal followed by a nice cup of coffee.

"I am out of stories that I can tell. The rest would most likely upset your readers." Benito said as he looked across the table to Ian.

"Thank you for your hospitality. I will send you a draft by tomorrow afternoon. After your approval, I will send it on to my editor," Ian said as he finished his coffee and stood up.

He was led back to the front door.

Ian was surprised to see that two cars were waiting.

He was taken to the lead car by the young man who had earlier escorted him.

This time Benito shook hands with Ian and said, "I am looking forward to your article."

"I'll send you all the material as promised. Later I will send you a first run copy of the newspaper," Ian replied truthfully.

He had every intent to do so. He was already thinking about how to get safely across the border.

Ian got into the back seat. Once again to his relief the young man got into the front seat.

Ian glanced back in time to see Benito getting into the car in back. Apparently, he had business back in town.

Ian's mind began to race and to envision a new scenario. Perhaps there would be an opportunity for his problem-solving on the way back to the highway.

He recalled one place ahead that would provide him with the opportunity he was seeking. Such a move would be dangerous, but it was the type of situation at which Ian excelled.

Ian silently opened his seat belt and prepared himself to act.

As the car took one sharp almost hair pin turn, around a small rise with a ravine on the left side of the car, Ian reached forward, grabbed the young man's chin with one hand and back of his head with the other. A quick twist ended his life.

Ian reached into the front pocket of the young man's suit and found the razor he had expected to find.

The driver was just reacting when Ian grabbed the steering wheel and twisted it to the left. Too late the driver realized the car was going to go over the edge and down into the canyon. He slammed on the brakes, but the momentum of the car would carry it over the edge.

Ian opened the back door, slit the driver's throat, and rolled out onto the rocky gravel road as the car disappeared.

He lay on the ground as the car behind came to a stop. Three doors opened, and three men approached him as Ian lay prone on the ground. He was on the edge of the road just shy of the drop down into the deep ravine.

The lead person was the very large guard who had searched him on arrival. As he reached down to turn Ian over, Ian grabbed the giant's wrist, put his right foot into his gut and hurled him over, head long down after the car.

The second person was just starting to raise his gun when Ian drove the pencil through his eye and into his head. Ian went swiftly around him toward Benito.

Benito was just raising his gun when Ian stepped in towards him, pushed his gun arm outward as the gun fired. The razor went across the back of the hand holding the gun, cutting all the tendons and the gun dropped to the ground.

There was a look of total surprise on Benito's face as Ian stepped past him as the razor slit his throat. By stepping past and behind him, Ian avoided the blood squirting out all around to the ground in front of Benito.

"Never talk. Carry out the required action and then breathe deeply," Ian recited his special forces instructor's saying.

The instructor had been a lifer that had softened just enough in his old age to become a decent trainer. In his spare time, Ian had learned and practiced every Aikido move useful in hand-to-hand combat.

Ian stepped past Benito and immediately verified there was no one else in the car.

Ian was looking for L-20. He had not seen him at the house. Ian figured that some other more important business had come up. Ian did not want to meet him anytime soon.

Ian threw the two bodies down the ravine where the giant grotesquely doubled over backwards on the top of the back bumper of the limo.

Ian closed all the doors on the still-idling second car and got in behind the wheel.

The total elapsed time for the problem-solving event was less than a minute. It seem like a life time and for some it had been.

Ian drove out of the lane at the same slow speed as before. He did not want to alert any guards that might be watching. He just hoped the fact that one car was missing would be totally overlooked by anyone looking out of the compound.

Ian drove a little faster once he was on the highway. Back in Nuevo Laredo, Ian parked the black car in the back corner of the Mac Donalds on the corner of Calle Venezuela and Cesar Lopez Avenue. Ian left the car running in hopes it would be recognized and since it was running it would keep people away.

Ian walked to the corner and flagged down a taxi.

Once back to the hotel, Ian walked across the lobby and took the elevator to his room. He made a quick check to ensure all his belongings were in his bag and two minutes later he was at the desk checking out.

He gave a small salute to Diego and went out to the cab that was waiting for him.

Ian took a taxi and headed to the shopping district at the foot of Bridge #1 that crossed over into the US.

The driver got the fair he asked for. Ian knew the driver was over charging and gave him a small tip. Ian hoped he would be quickly forgotten once the driver got a really good tip from some other gringo he had over charged.

There were a series of small booths selling "original and personally handmade dolls and other curios. Ian bought a small Mexican Doll.

He carried it for show and walked back across to the US. He thanked the border guard when the guard welcomed him back to the US after checking his passport.

A sigh of relief went through Ian as he went down the bridge steps to the corner of Salinas and Water streets.

He took a taxi back to the bus station and walked around it back to his car.

Ian smudged the front and back license plates. He was still in the disguise that he came across the bridge in. Ian got in and drove away from the back of the small bus station.

His destination was El Paso.

5 Recovery

*T*he snap of the broken neck, the stream of blood gushing like water from a garden hose, the giant guard folded backwards across the back bumper of the vertical limo down in the ravine, the second limo driver with a pencil through his eye, into his brain and finally the look of disbelief in Benito's eyes as his life pulsed out in a spray of blood, played out in an endless repeating loop in Ian's mind.

Benito's look of surprise had the greatest impact.

Benito's surprise had cost him his life. He should have been firing his gun long before Ian was able to disarm him and cut his throat with the straight razor.

Benito, who Ian had just finished interviewing and enjoying dinner with in what had been a delightful evening.

Benito who had told such delightful stories. Stories that were truly interesting.

Benito, who in those last few seconds of his life must have realized he had looked into the eyes of the devil.

Ian had originally planned to drive to San Antonio and take a bus that left at six in the morning for El Paso. Some premonition made him change his mind and he decided to drive.

He was still within the reach of Z-20. Ian was concerned that he might have the resources to watch airports and bus stations.

Ian decided the SUV was in good enough shape to make the trip with little problem if he held the speed down.

The constant replay of events was making it hard for him to concentrate on driving. He needed to stop somewhere soon.

He needed to take a hot shower and to take time to rest his exhausted mind and do something to let his guilty imagination remove the putrid stench of death that seemed to be lingering all around him.

Ian pulled into a rest stop long enough to search for a hotel up ahead and make a reservation. He noted he was still rational enough to look at several of the hotels his i-phone let him see.

He selected a hotel at Eagle Pass because of the picture of its workout room and what seemed to be a nice restaurant.

Rational criteria for an irrational crazy mind. The dark side of his brain was laughing. He wished he could go home where the bright light that Lesly exuded would push back the darkness. But home was not an option at this point on his trip.

Ian called and made reservations for two nights in the name of Robert Turan and gave the hotel the Amex card number.

It was lucky Ian engaged his GPS to guide him to the hotel. It got him onto state highway 83 and then brought him back from his self-torture long enough to get him on to 277 in Carrizo Springs.

Two hours later, mentally exhausted, Ian arrived at Eagle Pass and the hotel. The hotel foyer entrance appeared to Ian to be under a large rectangular white table with four blocky square legs. It was now almost midnight and the lights of the entrance guided Ian to its doors.

He parked his SUV in front of the four eight-foot-high vertical doors and stood for a moment next to the SUV before walking in. He needed a moment to gather himself and become the tired but friendly tourist from New Orleans.

He took a few moments to make sure he had the wallet belonging to one Robert Turan, a well-to-do descendant of the well-known Turan family. This was his new persona and he had to act the part.

The colorful orange couches, the pillows in the easy chair adjacent to the entrance, the bright lights, and the low whoosh of the two doors swinging swiftly open, all focused Ian's mind on getting registered.

For the moment he was in control as he walked up to the counter to face the smiling and for this time of night, too cheery clerk. Her white complexion, pixie cut blond hair and green eyes seemed out of place.

This was not Boston or New York but a small town of maybe twenty or thirty thousand in Texas, a stone's throw from the Mexican border. He had been expecting black hair, brown eyes, and tan skin.

Then her deep Texan drawl as she greeted Ian with a cheery *"Howdy"* coupled by the jeans and blue blouse with its top two buttons open, accented by a turquoise necklace transformed her to the out of place four pedaled bright yellow flower found in the spring on all the prickly pear cactus plants in Texas.

Standing barefoot Ian figured her to be five two but in her cowboy boots and her self-assured carriage she commanded the environment around her. Her name tag identified her as Katie.

Ian walked up to the registration counter greeted her with a *howdy Katie* in the best southern accent he could muster, stated his name, and presented his credit card. Ian got the smile he had been fishing for.

Here you are. Third floor, room 306, king size bed, work desk and business chair, couch, and kitchenette. You're all set.

She went on, "I always hate to ask but they tell me to, one key or two?"

"I only need one, when I lose that one, I will come for another," Ian replied.

He asked how late breakfast was served and was told ten.

Ian returned to his SUV and parked it in the nearest open spot. He pulled the plain dark blue soft sided suitcase with the name Robert Turan boldly printed in large black letters on a stainless-steel metal tag attached to the suitcase's woven top handle. He retrieved his backpack out of the back of the SUV and walked up to the two elevators and pressed the up button.

Ian stepped into the brightly lit interior as the right elevator doors opened immediately, as of course it would at the ungodly hour of twelve forty-five in the morning.

The elevator had a polished stainless-steel interior with a round oak wood railing that wrapped around at waist level. Ian turned to face the front and was surprised to come face to face with a stranger looking back at him from the closed elevator doors. He looked like hell.

The smooth slow ascent of the elevator identified it as a hydraulic lift type. Most people would be unaware of such minutiae, but Ian was always figuring out how the mechanical and electronic world around him worked. The doors opened slowly, and he stepped out.

He walked slowly down the yellow painted hallway, with its orange and tan patterned carpeting to Room 306 and placed the key card on the entrance lock. When the light turned green, he opened the door and turned on the room lights.

Cabinets with a microwave ran above a tan granite counter with a sink in the middle. A small refrigerator sat on the counter at the door end. Half of the left side of the entrance was a mirror, and the other half was a closet with sliding doors.

Ian slid the closet doors open. The entire interior was in white. An ironing board and iron hung on the right side. A metal suitcase stand was folded and leaned against the back wall. Three shelves with three small drawers below were on the left.

Ian opened the suitcase stand and put the suitcase on it. He put his backpack on the bottom shelf.

He then turned and stepped into the room onto the dark orange rug that seemed to have strings of light orange sperm swimming across the room toward the orange wall across from him. Ian wondered who would choose such a rug pattern?

The room was dominated by the white covered pistachio-green trimmed king size bed bracketed by lamps and oak bedside tables. It certainly caught the eye.

Above the couch facing the bed, two paintings of black, red, and grey hued desert sunsets added a sense that the couch was in a faceoff with the bed. The bed had large, long white pillows resting on a black headboard mounted on the wall and seemed to stare back across to the paintings in chaste innocence.

The scene led Ian to let out a chuckle as he fell, exhausted, across the bed. His mind was into wild interpretations of the simple world around him.

Ian awoke with a start as he mentally gathered his senses. He was stretched crosswise on the bed, still fully clothed. He had collapsed in both physical and mental exhaustion. He knew this was the aftereffects of the events of the day before. He looked at his phone to see that it was four forty-five in the morning.

Ian undressed and walked into the bathroom. The large walk-in shower stall featured a regular shower head and one hanging down from the ceiling. Ian began with the regular shower head.

The hot water spray on his face brought Ian slowly around. He felt much better. He switched to the overhead shower. He stood in the shower for a very long time. It was five thirty when he finally toweled off.

Once he had brushed his teeth and shaved. He was ready for a hearty breakfast.

The smell of sausage and bacon caused Ian to flash back to the events of the day before and then he recalled an event from his childhood.

He remembered a hard lesson he had learned as a boy about not getting too close to the animals that you would later put on the table as food. He had become attached to a runt pig that his dad had brought home. He had given the pig a name. The pig followed him around like a puppy. Eventually the piglet was a pig of butchering size. He tried to convince his dad to sell the pig instead of butchering him. The piglet ended up as bacon on the family table and was served for breakfast. The lesson, "don't get involved with the animal that is to be the meal."

He immediately flashed back to the events of the day before and the look of surprise on Benito's face. Ian had in a way gotten too attached.

Ian ate some sliced melon and a few grapes and left the breakfast area and the pancakes, eggs, and sausage. So much for my favorite breakfast, he thought.

He went to the small hotel exercise room with its single treadmill and universal weightlifting machine.

Ian spent the next two hours alternating between walking, jogging, and letting his mind process through its various emotions.

This was a harder lesson than the one he had learned as a boy on the farm. He would not repeat getting to know his target so personally again.

He took time to get ready for the next step of his journey.

Ian's focus switched to El Capitan of the Juarez cartel. El Capitan's location had been one of the hardest to find.

El Capitan's penchant for exercise and desire for the best equipment had been how Ian had "accidently or by luck" found out where he was located.

After El Capitan's son was arrested during a run in the park, El Capitan built his own gym inside his personal compound.

He had ordered the top line of Cybex exercise equipment.

Ian accidently learned of this through an acquaintance who liked to watch the show "The Biggest Loser" and had read on U tube that Vicente Carrillo Fuentes who was known as El Capitan had ordered the same equipment.

Ian contacted his support team and requested a search for the addresses of all equipment shipped to El Paso and Juarez. The next day the team identified a delivery company in Juarez where the equipment was sent. There was no local equipment delivery address online.

Ian would need to pay the delivery company a visit when he arrived in Juarez. They should have the delivery address in their files.

But he first had to get there.

It was time to be on his way, but he decided on one more day of rest and exercise. He would be ready when pancakes, with bacon and eggs were again palatable.

The following day after breakfast, he checked out of the hotel and made the several hour drive to a bed and breakfast located out on Purple Heart Boulevard in Juarez. This was the place he had sent many of the supplies he would need when he went on to San Diego.

He did not expect to use any of the supplies in Mexico.

The B&B owner recognized his name and said he had several boxes waiting back in the storage room. Ian asked him to keep them there for a couple days longer and made an excuse about visiting an army friend. He would ask for them before leaving.

Ian checked in, went to his room, and went to bed early.

<u>*6 El Paso-The Juarez Cartel*</u>

Juarez also long known by its old name as Paso del Norte, "Pass of the North," lay on the Mexican side of the river. El Paso on the US side with Juarez on the Mexican side made an almost perfect circle.

To the west the Sierra de Juarez mountains covered by a patch work of green and brown provided the southwest boundary. Franklin Mountain State Park poked its tip into the Northwestern part of El Paso.

Ian noted that Fort Bliss located in the middle of El Paso and Biggs Army Airfield provided the economic engine for the area.

The El Paso International airport took up the remainder of the Northwestern part of the greater El Paso area. El Paso, with a population of around seven hundred thousand, was actually the smaller of the two cities.

Juarez to the south in Mexico with more than a million people was a substantial and relatively modern city.

Ian chose to ride a bus into Mexico. This would reduce the risk of some accident exposing his presence. He would be the tourist looking for a quiet time. His hotel was a local low key one that offered personal family service. He did not want to utilize the more prominent and plush chain hotels.

The border guards on both sides of the border gave similar warnings.

"Have a good time but be careful, Juarez is a very dangerous place."

"No problem, I am only here for a couple of days of rest and relaxation." was Ian's reply.

Ian knew that his supplies had been delivered to the hotel in Juarez several weeks before.

Juarez was as modern city, perhaps more so than El Paso.

It appeared that the morning rush hour was nearing the end as he easily flag down a cab and gave the driver the hotel address.

He noticed new construction seemed to be everywhere. Juarez was enjoying robust growth and good economic times.

The ride had taken him away from the hustle and bustle of the town center. He seemed to have entered an area where working people made their homes.

The hotel located on a corner had the look of a double deck storage box rental building that was surrounded by an eight-foot-high wall. It was certainly not one of the high-rise, glittery western tourist hotels.

His team had responded to his request that his accommodations should be discrete and be one that locals would frequent. He hoped they had chosen well.

The plain cement courtyard was edged by red flowers and some small cactus plants that rose up through a layer of pebbles.

The hotel owner was very gracious and said Ian's boxes were already in the room he had requested. He stated that dinner was served at six in a family style setting in the dining room just behind the office area.

Ian thanked him, accepted his key card, and walked toward the end opposite the main office. He had a large end room near the quiet street.

The room was surprisingly spacious and bright. The yellow curtains stood out against the light brown color of the walls. The bed cover was embroidered with the symbol of the Mexican Eagle on a cactus with a snake in its beak. It was a tastefully done décor.

This was to be home for the next few days.

Ian checked out the supply boxes. They were unopened and everything seemed to be in order.

Ian put his things away. On this problem-solving outing he did not expect to have his room examined.

He was hungry and ready for a late breakfast, so he proceeded to go down to get his family style meal.

The dining room was a spacious area with several large tables made of at least four-inch-thick dark brown wood. It was finished in a clear glaze that seemed to be at least one-half inch thick.

The large chairs were of the same dark wood and were finished in the same clear glaze. The chair cushions were embroidered with different flowers.

Ian enjoyed the cozy feel of a place where friends gathered for their meals.

"Breakfast is offered starting at six in the morning. You are welcome to close the breakfast period. You must let me know if you want lunch," the owner informed him.

After breakfast, Ian walked across the hotel courtyard to a black wrought iron gate next to the main entry gate of the same design. He heard the lock open as he put his card up to the lock.

He walked out and turned left and walked toward where his map showed a local pottery shop that was located about four blocks away.

The street was a mix of individual homes and small businesses. The houses seemed well kept and their yellow, red, and tan exteriors seemed to have been coordinated. It was a giant mosaic made by the color of each home.

The effect was to make one smile and feel good.

The shop he went into was a combination cement, brick, roof tile and garden material supplier. It was much larger than the front implied. The front was equivalent to a four-car garage in width, but the depth was at least one hundred feet.

Ian walked past bags of cement and specialty stones. He could see out to a large back area that was stacked with bricks and tile.

One of the store's specialties was to make garden ornaments and objects to order. Ian sketched out a picture of an eight by eight by four-inch-thick block with a cone depression on one side that went down for two inches with a small hole through the center of the block.

"I would like two dozen of these blocks," Ian said as he showed the sketch to the shop owner.

The owner speaking in Spanish asked how the blocks would be used.

"Esto es fácil de hacer. ¿Para qué es esto?" the store owner inquired.

"It is for a garden landscape project. I will have water coming up into each cone. Can you make it from clay," was Ian's inquiring reply?

"Esto es simple, no hay problema," the owner replied.

Ian planned to pack the cones in each block with C4. The cone shape would function to focus the explosive force outward in a tight pattern.

Ian anticipated using them but was not sure exactly where or how many he needed.

He first needed to find the exact location of El Capitan. He could then finalize his solution approach and know exactly how many explosives were needed.

Ian's next stop was to go to the address of the exercise equipment shop that had delivered the exercise equipment to El Capitan. There he hoped to obtain the address that he needed.

He walked back to his hotel and caught a cab. The cab ride to the delivery address took about forty-five minutes.

Out of the cab window Ian saw a sign with Los Pablos's in big red letters. The restaurant's stylized blue peacock with yellow eyes with a dark blue center was accompanied by Los Pablos's No. 4 across the rest of the window.

A huge Hospital loomed directly behind it and in front of the restaurant, across the street was another medical facility.

It made sense that a concern in the business of selling exercise equipment was located in this area.

Ian decided that lunch would be a good idea. He went into the restaurant and ordered two beef tongue tacos with refried beans. This was a favorite taco that he normally only found in Mexico.

"Me sorprende que sé cómo comer lengua de vaca," the young waitress commented.

"Crecí en una granja," Ian replied in Spanish explaining that he had grown up on a farm and had learned to eat beef tongue when he was a young boy.

After lunch Ian walked out of the restaurant and turned to his left.

The equipment sales and delivery store was only two buildings away on the same side of the street. He walked by scanning the building for cameras.

He crossed the street and took in the entire red brick, two story structure that had about one hundred fifty-foot presence along the street.

It was a big place.

There were no visible cameras, but all the windows and doors had strong steel bars across them.

The other buildings did not seem to have any external cameras either.

Ian decided that everything he was seeing was good for him.

The only downside to the area was that it was well lit. It would be hard to walk up to the front of the building and not be seen.

Ian saw a driveway at the end of the building on his walk past the store.

The lot next to the driveway was empty.

Just past the lot was a sports bar.

Ian decided that an afternoon beer at the bar would be appropriate.

From the bar Ian was able to study the back part of the sports equipment building. He had what he needed because he now knew how to get into the building.

Ian called his cab which appeared almost instantly. The driver had parked in the restaurant parking lot.

"Back to the hotel," Ian instructed in Spanish.

The hotel shower was a large plain square covered in white tile with a thin black tile edging around the top. The hot shower relaxed Ian. He enjoyed the wide spray from the large shower head. He felt guilty about how much water he was using. He stood a long time under the hot water. He realized he was still recovering from his last solution.

By the time he had dried off and dressed it was time for dinner.

Ian locked his room and walked to the other end of the hotel to enjoy the evening meal.

After dinner, Ian made sure to call a different cab and instructed it to drop him off at the Hospital. Ian took up a slow jog on the sidewalk that went along the chain link fence that surrounded the hospital parking lot.

There were no other people out.

The restaurant was still open, and a few patrons were sitting inside. The sporting goods store was dark. The lights for the sports bar were on but no one was outside.

Ian turned and jogged back into the back-parking lot of the sporting goods store and then stopped.

He went to the truck loading dock hoping to find an easy way in.

Ian checked for and found that the store did have an older contact alarm system. Each door and window had a matching contact on the fixed surface. Breaking the contact between the two would set off the alarm.

This was an easy security system for Ian to work around.

His next concern was whether a motion detection system had been installed as a way to back up the older contact system.

Ian spotted what was probably a camera system. He would incapacitate it with a bright spotlight once he got in the door.

He got on his back, and very slowly opened the door.

He was looking up to see if there was a motion sensor.

He verified that there was.

He took a small bag and what folks were now calling a collapsible selfy handle and very slowly raised the bag and slipped it over the camera. If checked before it recycled there would only be black in the system.

Ian hoped this place still used a continuous tape system and not the newer digital system with memory storage.

Once in Ian used the same routine in the other two rooms in the front office area. He did not expect to go into the warehouse and loading dock area.

He wished he could have thanked the filing clerk. He or she was very organized, and Ian was able to find the information he needed in less than ten minutes.

Ian put the address on a sticky note that he found on the very neat desk with everything in its place.

It had taken thirty minutes to break in. It took a little longer to break out. It seemed to him he had gotten in and out undetected.

Ian jogged back to the hospital and took a cab back to the hotel.

The next morning after breakfast, Ian took a cab to an address several blocks away from the one on the sticky note.

It was clear to Ian that El Capitan lived in an exclusive part of the city.

Ian walked casually along the tree lined street to a cluster of new high-rise buildings.

The shops with their single purses, single pairs of shoes on widely spread shelves made it clear that these were up-scale boutiques selling upscale products.

Across a small cobblestone square the address on his sticky note was boldly emblazoned in large brass letters on the gate to a walled compound. To the left of the gate, there was a building with what appeared to be a gun tower on the flat roof. Ian took the building to be where the guards would be located.

Getting in would be a challenge. Getting out alive would require some major distraction.

Ian slowly walk causally by.

He spotted an internet café and decided he could get a closer look from a Google vantage point. He bought a cup of coffee and time on one of the computers. With Google, he got a view from above of the compound and the area around it. The back wall had a ravine running close by behind it. The compound walls were ten feet high with razor wire along the tops. There was another guard tower on the far back corner of the compound.

It was clear to Ian that he would not be able to climb in over any of the walls.

He would need to find another way in.

An idea for a major distraction came to Ian and he decided on a reconnaissance of the back wall. He was sure there would be a camera system. He needed to determine if it had a blind spot.

Ian left the internet café and walked toward the tallest building in the area. Perhaps he could utilize it to get a better view of the compound.

The black car parked just around the corner on the street off the square immediately caught Ian's attention. Though the windows were tinted, the car seemed to be occupied.

Ian changed his mind about the building and entered the restaurant that occupied the entire corner of the block. The smartly set tables with their white napkins folded into swans sitting on the black tablecloth with white placement clothes declared it as an upscale place.

Ian knew he was not dressed properly but proceeded boldly in.

He asked for a table by the side windows. While studying the menu, he watched as two "men in black" got out of the car and walked to the single, white metal door on the side of the building that had been Ian's goal. A few moments later two similarly dressed men came out, got in the car, and drove away.

As the black car drove away, a grey ford slowly made a U-turn from the curb and followed the black one.

Ian realized that the men in the black car were being watched by those in the grey car. It was not clear who was watching who. But there seemed to be too many watchers. He was not sure if the authorities were watching the compound and if the cartel was keeping tab of who was using the building. Or it could be the other way around. In either case, the building was too hot to use.

Getting in and out of the compound had just become a bigger challenge.

Ian relaxed as his chicken salad lunch arrived.

He recalled the beggar sitting on the sidewalk looking out onto the square. He had dropped a ten-peso coin into the beggar's hat.

An idea came to him.

He ordered a soft drink and steak sandwich to go.

After finishing his lunch Ian exited the restaurant and walked back into the square.

He slowed his pace to get a better look at the beggar. Ian was aware at how little attention one paid to the actual looks of a beggar. The body odor became noticeable at about a ten-foot distance. This alone would make people take a wider berth around the beggar.

The feeling of personal guilt was immediate. Ian approached and squatted down next to the cross-legged beggar. The beggar was about Ian's size. His hat out in front of him was the receptacle for the meager donations.

"Cual es su nombre?" Ian inquired the beggar's name.

"Jorge"

"Jorge, here is a beef sandwich and a soft drink for your lunch.

"Gracias," was the only word Jorge uttered as he looked at Ian.

"¿me vender tu ropa," Ian asked.

He asked if the beggar would sell him his clothes and if he would like a nice place to stay for a few weeks.

"Why would you offer such a thing," Jorge questioned?

"I lost a bet, and I must live like a beggar for a week," Ian lied to him.

"Ok, why me," he asked as he took a bite of the sandwich.

"Because you are the right size and you were sitting in a place that seems safe," Ian replied.

"Si, it is the most watched square in the city," the beggar replied.

"OK, where is this vacation place you are offering and for how long do I get to stay," Jorge continued as he took a swig of the soft drink.

"It will be at the Inn at Ciudad Juarez for two weeks. Golf will be at Club Campestre," Ian replied.

Ian knew that the hotel was a grand place. He was also aware that were several great restaurants around the hotel.

"For four weeks, several rounds of golf each week and free meals and you can have my clothes and my spot," he bargained.

"Well now you are getting greedy. I may need to find a different beggar that doesn't play golf. How about three weeks, two rounds of golf each week, all the food you want to eat, and I will set you up in some new clothes that make you fit in," Ian countered.

"Oh, and you have to tell me where you go to the bathroom or go to get something to eat when you are in the square." Ian countered.

Ian knew he could have let Jorge have exactly what he wanted but the bargaining was part of making the deal.

"Jorge, I am going to walk around the corner. Wait a few moments and meet me there," Ian instructed as he got up and walked slowly down the street.

Ian called a cab. Jorge and the cab arrived almost in unison.

Ian instructed the cab driver to go to a shopping center. There Ian bought Jorge several casual but very nice outfits. Ian included a sports jacket, a regular pair of shoes and some golf shoes. The beggars outfit went into some plastic bags.

Jorge walked out looking like a new person. Next, they stopped and bought a suitcase. Then at a pharmacy they bought personal hygiene products.

It was clear that the Inn located just north of the Campestre Golf Club was relatively new. Ian had chosen to offer it since it was so close to the golf course.

He had called in to his support team to make the reservation and to arrange for access to the golf course. The cab stopped at the front entrance below the massive entrance cover that once again reminded Ian of two tables stacked on top of each other.

Two porters opened the doors to let them out of the cab. Ian paid the cab driver, gave him a good tip, and asked him if he could wait for a few moments.

The two receptionists looked up as Jorge and Ian approached. Ian inquired about a suite with one king-size bed. He gave his name.

"Si, we made the reservation only an hour ago. You were lucky the executive suite you asked for was available. It has been reserved for the next three weeks."

Ian inquired about the payment.

"It has all been taken care of. Also, the money you requested to be made available has been transferred to the room account," she continued.

"Jorge, I hope you have good time. You have an honorary membership to the Golf club. It turns out that you can play every day if you wish. It is all part of the membership. You have a daily spending allowance of one hundred dollars and your room is paid for," Ian said as he got ready to leave.

"Ah, this is indeed a wonderful vacation. I hope my clothes and location work for you," Jorge said as he took the key card for his room and followed the porter toward the elevator.

Ian looked around the grand lobby, thanked the receptionist and walked out to his waiting taxi.

Ian returned to his hotel room with Jorge's smelly clothes. He wished he could clean them but decided against doing so. Ian shook out the clothes, put them on hangers and hung them on the shower curtain rail. He used some soap and water to wipe the inside of the shoes and the inside of the sombrero.

He would need to be just as repulsive as Jorge had been. The only thing he would do different was to use a cardboard box to collect the money anyone might give him. Ian would be hiding under the large sombrero Jorge had use to serve this function.

Ian washed his hands and went to have some dinner. A bottle of Madero was really an attractive thought.

After dinner he put on his jogging clothes and took a cab out to the compound area. He had chosen an address about one half mile away. He asked the driver to return in two hours to pick him up. He turned as if to walk up to the house he was standing in front of. Once the cab departed, he slowly jogged toward the compound area.

He went down into the drain ravine and came slowly up where it was the closest to the corner of the compound. He pulled on his camouflage top and then slowly crawled on his belly to the corner of the compound wall.

The cameras were fixed and were pointed along the top of the razor wire. It appeared that there was a blind spot along the base of the wall.

Ian wanted to make sure it was really a blind spot. He crawled along the base of the wall from one end to the other and then crawled back.

Nothing happened. Verification was complete.

He then went into the ravine and got out of his camouflage top and carefully went back to the point where the cab would pick him up.

Early the next morning after breakfast, Ian walked to the garden shop and picked up the blocks he had ordered on his arrival.

The shop owner greeted him as he walked in and showed him the twenty-four blocks. Ian examined them and thanked the owner for doing such a good job. He paid for all twenty-four but asked if he could leave twelve of them to be picked up later.

Ian packed the other twelve blocks carefully into his backpack. It was clear the load was at the maximum weight that he could carry. Ian staggered out of the shop and slowly made his way back to the hotel. He put the backpack into the hotel room closet.

It was time to go begging.

Ian dressed in Jorge's well-worn clothes and tried to make himself look as close as possible to the local beggar. He was sure he would stand out like a sore thumb, but this seemed to be the only option.

He had the cab driver drop him off just outside the square. Ian walked slowly out and sat down on the corner where he had found Jorge. He put his sign asking for donations in the small cardboard box and then leaned back against the wall with the sombrero on his head.

Ian realized that no one seemed to notice the difference in the beggar. He received a few coins and quietly thanked each of his contributors in Spanish.

It was hard to ask for money for breakfast or for lunch or for any reason. He came to realize how difficult it was to beg and even more difficult to sit in one place for so long. His backside hurt after the first day.

After three days, Ian had enough understanding about El Capitan's routine. El Capitan left early in the morning and returned in the early afternoon and then stayed in for the rest of the night.

The only other regular traffic in and out of the compound seemed to be the people that worked for El Capitan, a variety of delivery vehicles and the garbage truck. Delivery was done at the gate. Only the garbage truck was allowed in each day.

The garbage truck was one of those round bodied compression trucks that crushed the garbage that was dumped in. The procedure at the gate was for the garbage truck to stop at the gate and cycle through the compression cycle before being let in through the gate. It appeared that the same garbage truck came every day in the morning.

Ian realized that unlike the movies with their underground tunnel entrances, his only way in would be in the back of the garbage truck.

Ian had also paid close attention to the other people who were watching the compound and the people who were watching the watchers. He would need to set up a way to distract all of them.

On the last morning that Ian was planning to spend in the square, he brought several especially prepared radio-controlled explosive packs. He wandered past the cars on the side street and placed the charges on lamp posts that were near where the watcher's cars were located and one on the door used by the watchers in the building.

Ian had located the window to the room on the fourth level that was being used to watch the compound. He scaled up an inside corner of the building and went in an open room window and out to the hotel hallway. He walked cautiously down the hallway and placed his final charge above the doorway of the room the watchers were in.

Ian's plan was to distract the watchers. He had no desire to hurt anyone. His charges would do some damage but mostly they would just be loud, release a cloud of gas, be a surprise and cause confusion.

Ian spent the next three days following the garbage truck and learning where it was parked overnight.

He then went to a hardware store and rented an acetylene torch, a drill and bought some hinges and latches.

Ian spent most of the night modifying the inside of the garbage truck so he could step through the compression gate when it cycled and so he could get out the bottom when he was inside the compound.

Ian practiced opening the door that would allow him to step through the compression plunger as it cycled back and forth.

He also made several small holes in the side of the container, so he would be able to utilize his flexible optics to see where the driver and his helper were and what they were doing.

It was time to prepare the main distraction event at the compound.

Ian spent the next day in his room packing the dozen shaped charges with C4 and carefully inserting the small radio-controlled triggers through the holes in the block.

That evening he crawled along the back wall of El Capitan's compound and placed each charge at the foot of each wall pillar.

Ian took the time to hide the evidence of his digging and arranged the area to make his handiwork unnoticeable.

There were nine charges in all. Ian hoped the explosion would topple the entire back wall.

The toppling of the wall was purely a distraction to allow his escape in the opposite direction.

It was past three in the morning before he was retreating back into the drain ravine.

Ian was not through. He proceeded to where the garbage truck was parked for the night with his three extra explosives. He also carried his inside the compound mission backpack. He climbed into the back of the garbage truck.

He sat down and fell asleep.

The roar of the truck engine brought Ian out of his brief sleep. He was instantly on the alert. He hoped that the driver would not cycle the plunger immediately.

Ian poked his flexible camera out of the truck's side so he could see where they were going.

He was pleased that it appeared the truck was going to the compound first. That made sense since this allowed the guard to see an empty truck.

Ian was dressed in his camouflage gear and would be hard to see. The guard had not looked into the compartment before, and Ian hoped that the previous practice would be followed.

The truck came in through a gate to the side of the control room building.

It went through the compression cycle.

It then proceeded to the back of the compound.

Ian realized that the easiest exit was out the back of the truck. The garbage was loaded into the truck up front from the side. The back of the truck was about a foot from the back wall.

One of the garbage men rolled out one the large containers from the holding area. The truck mounted forklift system was lowered, and the container rolled onto the forks.

Ian patiently waited for the large container to begin its upward journey.

One operator was looking at the controls and the other with his back to him was looking up at the slowly moving container.

Ian put his hands around his two bags, got out the back of the truck and darted behind the main garbage area gates. He was relieved to find a small side door leading into the compound garbage holding area.

Inside there were two designated areas for the containers and there was one recycling area.

Imagine, a Mexican drug lord that was conscientious about recycling!

Ian crawled in behind the recycle bins. When the first big bin was put back in its place, he changed location and hid behind it.

The second big bin was emptied and returned.

The recycle was taken and put on the back of the truck.

The two men closed the garbage area and slowly drove away.

Ian was in, but he now had to wait until dark for his next step.

He was hoping to get into the exercise area before El Capitan returned.

The time in the trash bin area was put to use locating all the surveillance cameras. Ian's fiber optic eye at the end of a cable allowed him to look over the wall and study every inch of his surroundings. He hoped to get to the gym unnoticed.

Late in the afternoon a person that looked like one of the cooks came out from the house to dump some trash.

Once he entered the trash bin area, Ian knocked him out. He would have a terrible headache but would likely live to complain about his ordeal. Ian taped him up with duct tape and put him into the large garbage container. He would wake up later bound and gagged but he would be able to free himself with some effort.

Ian wished himself luck as he put on the cook's outfit and made the best adjustment to himself so he would appear to be the cook.

He then walked slowly back looking down and away from the cameras. He had put all of the needed supplies into a body vest. He carried his three extra explosive blocks as if they were cakes. He hoped the guards were not being vigilante about monitoring one of the cooks.

Once inside, Ian looked up the well-lit hallway trying to decide where to go.

He was relieved to find no additional technology facing him. He took his best guess at the location of the gym and headed that way.

His senses were at full alert. He was peeking furtively into doorways and was ready to attack anyone he met.

Luck is always the best ally. Ian opened a door and was rewarded with the sight of a series of Cybex exercise machines. He quickly stepped in and closed the door behind him. There was no one in the gym area.

A steam bath and a sauna were on the other side of the room. Ian moved immediately to the sauna and the steam room. Both were empty.

Behind the sauna was a hot water whirlpool big enough for a dozen people. It had a foot-wide ledge all the way around the pool.

Ian strategically placed his explosives. One would take out the steam room and the other would take out the sauna. The third he put in the corner besides the entrance door. He hoped it would go unnoticed.

The ledge around the hot water pool was a perfect place to wait. Ian could stand in the corner and remain unseen even if several men accompanied El Captain into the room.

Ian envisioned and worked through several scenarios that he might face. He hoped El Capitan indeed was an evening exerciser. It would be much easier to leave in the dark than in the light of day.

Ian continued to play through several exit scenarios.

He came to full alert as the door to the exercise area opened. He heard someone say "clear." Next, he heard the treadmill begin to operate.

Ian kept his eyes open but relaxed in the corner of the hot tub. He was breathing evenly and in a set rhythm. He was ready for hand-to-hand action if necessary.

Sometime later he heard, "Is the steam room hot?"

Ian was now at full ready. He could see a hand and arm as the control dial was turned.

"Make sure the sauna is ready. Get me out of the steam room in fifteen minutes."

"Fifteen minutes," someone repeated.

Ian heard the door to the steam room open and close. He put in his ear plugs, put on his thin leather gloves, and then moved into action.

Ian moved quickly but quietly. He looped the choke wire around the guard's throat as the door to the steam room closed. A quick jerk locked the wire in place. He sent the guard sliding out into the workout area ahead of him.

The second guard was just pulling his gun when the choke wire locked around his throat.

Ian pulled both guards over to the water cooler. They were already dead.

It was not a fair way to fight but the circumstance required the actions he was taking. Fair was not a requirement.

As Ian stood back up, the door to the steam room opened and El Capitan came out with his gun drawn.

Ian immediately understood how this man had survived so long.

"Vas a morir…," El Capitan began to shout.

Ian pressed one of the control buttons.

The explosion in the sauna, and the steam room hurtled Ian into the wall behind him. El Capitan was sliced into a thousand pieces by the shattered glass from the steam room door and the sauna.

Dazed but alive Ian went into an adrenaline high slow-motion action mode. He could feel some blood running down his nose.

He pressed a second control button.

He was sure the first explosions would have kicked off some sort of reaction but the explosions along the rear wall would awaken the entire compound and the surrounding neighborhood.

Ian picked up his final charge and left the exercise area and went toward the front of the house. He looked out the front window and saw a small army of men heading for the front door and another contingent heading around the side of the house.

He immediately exited out the side door to the other side of the hedge. He ran toward the front gate behind the bushes on the edge of the driveway. The guards ran past him on the building side.

His goal was the electrical substation that he saw ahead of him and to the left of the entrance gate.

He opened the gate to the substation and taped a charge to the main transformer. He lay down at the roots of the hedge. He pushed another two buttons on his control panel.

The shock and the noise of the explosion stunned him.

The bushes around him ceased to exist.

"Keep moving," his internal control system said as he listened to a whistling sound and figured some part of the transformer was coming down from above.

The second button that Ian had pushed set off the two bombs planted near the watchers that were out on the other side of the square.

Ian hoped the observers were now too busy trying to figure out what was happening to them to worry about what was happening in the compound.

At the entrance gate Ian slapped on another charge.

He stepped to the side to blast the gates open. At almost the same time the very large top from the transformer landed in the exact spot along the bushes where he had been just a moment before.

"Damn," flashed through his mind as he triggered the charge on the gates.

A single guard sat at the control panel. He stood up with a stunned look on his faced as Ian stumbled into the gate house control center.

Ian hit him in the throat and the guard went down gagging. Ian immediately placed his last charge on the control consul.

He stepped back and stripped the jumpsuit off and put on the wig and beard hoping to make himself look like the beggar frequenting the corner across the square.

The guard still had a pulse, so Ian did his one good deed of the evening and pulled him out of the building and halfway across the square.

He could hear the police sirens and just caught the lights in his peripheral vision as he pressed the last button to trigger the charge in the gate house. The windows and doors blew out. Once again, he found himself hurdled back on his butt.

He knew he would be sore the next day.

The police swarmed into the compound.

"Get out of here old man," one of the officers told him as he helped Ian up and gave him a push away from the compound. Another policeman was attending to the guard on the ground. An ambulance came roaring in as Ian made it to the street corner where the beggar normally sat.

He just kept walking. After several blocks he caught a cab back to the hotel.

The next morning every bone in his body seemed to ache. A long hot shower helped. After breakfast, Ian took a taxi back to the main bus station and caught a bus back across the border into the US.

He retrieved his SUV that he had put into secure monitored storage to ensure none of the gear he needed for San Diego would be stolen.

He left El Paso and about an hour later stopped for lunch.

The morning news was about a mysterious explosion that had destroyed the compound of one of the wealthy community leaders. The leader had died in the fire.

<u>*7 San Diego Launch*</u>

Ian had selected San Diego as the launch location for the strike against the Tijuana Cartel. He had located the Cartel's headquarters in a waterfront warehouse in the Ensenada basin harbor located on the Baja peninsula. He figured that getting there by sea made the most sense.

The warehouse was located just across the harbor from the Mexican Navy base. Ian was sure some high-ranking officer in the Navy was getting a healthy addition to his government pay. There could be no other explanation for the cartel to locate so close to a military base.

The drive to San Diego provided some of the decompression time he needed. His GPS put the direct drive at ten hours and eighteen minutes. Ian figure it would be more like twenty hours. He would stop on the way for another hot shower to relieve his aching body.

Ian laughed to himself when he realized the town of Eloy was the most likely place to stop. He recalled the story of The Time Machine by HG Wells. The Eloi were the gentler surface victims of the underground sinister Morlocks. He thought he would probably be a Morlock if he had been in the story. He decided it was appropriate for him to stop at Eloy.

Again, he laughed at his own bad joke.

The terrain around Eloy was sand, with sparse patches of grasses, some that had some green and other patches dead and dry.

The overall feeling was one of a dry, desolate land where life struggled to take hold and repeatedly lost the battle.

Eloy was on Interstate 10. It was a few miles before hitting Interstate 8 that went west to San Diego. Ian got off the exit prior to the town.

Ian's critical eye really made him feel like a Morlock.

The hotel had an empty fountain with a blue center piece where the water should come flowing out. It was clear to him that conserving the water was more important than having a working fountain. The expanse of small gravel around the fountain was carefully raked into wave-like patterns spread around gardens of larger stone flower beds.

The light blue roof of the Inn was accented by the darker blue posts of the veranda on the first and second floors. The parking lot was totally empty. He figured he would have no problems getting a room.

Ian almost reconsidered his choice but decided that he could stand it for one night. He parked near the lobby entrance.

He looked around and wondered what the entertainment of the younger crowd would be in an area like this. It had to be bars and night clubs. He wondered where they were located.

The receptionist was a motherly looking middle aged, slightly overweight woman. Betty was written in black across a white well used name tag pinned to her blouse. Ian guessed Betty to be in the late forties or early fifties.

Betty was pleasant and seemed pleased that he had chosen the American Inn.

Ian asked for a room with a King-sized bed preferably on the second floor.

"I have one in the back where it will be quiet," Betty replied without even looking on her computer screen. Ian wondered where any noise might possibly come from.

Ian decided against dinner and chose to take a long, long hot shower.

His body was one big bruise. He had a cut on his forehead and had removed a few pieces of glass from his right cheek. He knew where and how he had gotten his various injuries, but he had never felt any of it until he was driving. The aches seemed to surface as his mind went over everything that he had gone through so far.

He decided it was not a very good idea to put himself in the middle of exploding C4 or to rely on only his explosive being the ones that would be around to explode.

He stood under the shower and let the hot water hit his backside. He whispered an Oh! and Ah! as he slowly turned and let the hot water run down his body. He would have loved to sit down in a hot tub and just lounge in the comfort of the hot water.

After the shower Ian made himself a cup of coffee.

He went smoothly and slowly through his Tae Kwon Do moves as he listened to the news and periodically sipped his coffee. He counted one hundred push-ups and then collapsed in a verbal groan.

His mind became focused on his next target. It seemed the route he had designed was constantly pitting him against the next more dangerous cartel. Each time he seemed to be going up one rung on the danger ladder. In the coming confrontation perhaps, it was not more dangerous but more bizarre.

This cartel was known to have dissolved over three hundred of their rivals in fifty-gallon barrels of sodium hydroxide.

He was sure those going into the drums were tortured first.

He hoped that dissolving was done after the person was dead. If not, then he figured this was one mean and nasty cartel.

Ian told himself to get this one right and not end up in one of their sodium hydroxide drums.

"This will be another explosive foray," he thought as he contemplated and thought through the next scenario. This time he would make sure he was not around when the explosives went off.

By nine thirty he was ready for bed. He was asleep as his head hit the pillow.

Ian awoke at five thirty in the morning. He got up, dressed, and went down to check out.

Betty had been replaced by Fred. They both seemed to have the same well used name tags. He wondered when they would be replaced.

When he asked about breakfast, Fred suggested Denny's as the preferred place. It was also conveniently located at the entrance to I 10. Ian thanked Fred and walked out to the SUV.

Ian drove to Denny's ready for a hearty breakfast and a cup of coffee.

He was rested and ready to get to San Diego to the Seaside Marina located near Sea World.

The drive was long enough for him to go through the entire upcoming solution scenario.

Four hours later Ian was pleased to be greeted by an increase in the number of cars as he neared San Diego. He had driven straight through lunch and was now getting into the San Diego region in the early afternoon just prior to the rush hour.

US I8 came to an end at the San Diego, Sea World Park area at Sea World Drive. Ian got off the drive and onto Quivira Way and located the Seaside Boat rentals office. He parked out in front of the office and went in.

When Ian inquired about the Whistling Nanny, the manager came out of his office to greet him.

"I am Tim Cocaine. And let's skip over the drug jokes. I understand that you are here to inspect your rental, the Whistling Nanny," Tim introduced himself.

Tim was a slender well-tanned body with sun bleached brown hair and looked to Ian like a surfer.

"Yes, I am, and I will skip all the jokes, but you might catch me chuckling a couple of times," Ian replied as he shook Tim's hand.

Ian took a liking to Tim's open and what seemed to be direct manner.

"Captain Bitterly," Tim began.

Ian smiled as Tim formally used Ian's new identity.

"I won't make fun of your name if you call me Matt instead of Captain Bitterly," Ian cut Tim off.

"Matt, the owner is really happy about this thirty-day rental. It is a very attractive deal. However, she personally asked me to make certain you know how to handle the Whistling Nanny," Tim went on.

Ian had rented the Whistling Nanny for thirty-days at two thousand dollars a day plus a hundred-thousand-dollar deposit. The Nanny was one of the better yachts available for rent.

Ian followed Tim out of the office and then along the pier. The Nanny was immediately noticeable. She was the largest vessel in the bay and moored parallel to the pier's right-hand side.

The two walked out toward her. The late afternoon sun still had several hours to reach the horizon.

The afternoon sun was reflecting off the Whistling Nanny's white side with a black strip in an almost blinding display of elegance.

Matt led the way onto the boat.

"Your supplies arrived a day ago. We can bring them down whenever you want," Tim commented as the two walked aboard.

The selection of the make and model of the Nanny came from his previous experience in dealing with the pirates off the coast of Africa. It was a Bavarian Cruiser that he had crewed on. His mission then was to put a hit on the pirates in that area. Ian had learned how to handle this boat under extreme learning conditions, and he knew the cruiser's capabilities. He had learned how to make it dance for him. He had come to love its capability and ease of handling. He hoped the Nanny would handle in the same manner.

Ian thoroughly inspected the Nanny. Ian was no sea captain and not an expert, but he wanted to see what condition the boat was in.

The Bavarian Cruiser was a luxury vessel with three spacious bedrooms. Two bedrooms located toward the back had queen-size beds and plenty of the living area and the third bedroom where Ian planned to sleep, and just as nice as the back two, was in the bow and featured a king-size bed.

The spacious kitchen with a gas stove and a sink was separated from a booth and table eating area by a stand-up countertop. A black leather couch with two companion chairs with fixed small end tables rounded out the general relaxation area that was in the middle of the main deck.

Ian was as impressed with the Nanny as he had been previously with the same craft in Africa. He took the time to inspect the immaculate engine compartment, the sail holds and all the rigging.

"I have got to know why she is called the Whistling Nanny," Ian asked Tim.

"It's a great story," Tim began with a chuckle.

"The current owner ended up with the boat as part of the divorce settlement with her husband. Her nanny had a romantic affair with the husband. The nanny felt guilty and admitted it all. The wife then took every penny her husband had in the divorce. She bought the boat and periodically sailed it up and down the coast while her kids were growing up. Her nanny became her deck hand, and the boat was renamed the Whistling Nanny," Tim shared.

Ian judged the Whistling Nanny just as luxurious as had been promised and it was in excellent shape.

"I like her looks, can I take her out for a trial run," Ian asked.

"Sure, if you don't mind me acting as your deck hand. I have instructions to verify your capability in handling the boat before letting you take her for the month.

I can connect you with some good deck hands if you want," Tim replied.

Thanks for the offer. My deck hands will be here the day after tomorrow. Let's take her for a quick run.

Ian removed the covers from the main sails and went forward to make sure the spinnaker was ready. The rigging was all automated and controlled from the control panel in front of the main rudder wheel.

Cast the lines loose," Ian said as the diesel engine purred to life.

Ian backed the Nanny slowly away from the pier and pointed her bow toward the harbor exit. They went smoothly out of the harbor using the diesel engine. He could have sailed her out, but he did not want to alarm Tim or make him think he liked hot dogging. Ian stayed on the diesel until he had left the channel. Then he turned toward the south, so he could catch the wind.

As the sail filled Ian turned off the engine. The Nanny responded like an eager dog pulling on the leash. It was clear to Ian she wanted to fly.

"I can feel her come to life and say thank you. It's been too long," Ian voiced his thoughts.

"She was out only two weeks ago," the Tim replied.

"So, you agree with the Nanny," Ian said with a smile as the head sail reached the top of the mast and the Nanny responded with new energy.

The Whistling Nanny began to earn her name as she seemed to leap forward with new life. The lines of the yacht were literally whistling.

"This is the first time I have been on her when the head sail was in use. I didn't know she could move this fast," Tim shouted.

"Going faster doesn't mean you have to speak louder," Ian said in a normal voice as he smiled at Tim.

Ian knew the exhilaration Tim was feeling because he was feeling the rush of elation energizing his soul like the cream sauce in a Fettuccine Alfredo gave life to the spaghetti.

It all tasted so good.

His soul found release.

For the moment life was pure.

Ian sailed the Nanny out about a mile and then turned and sailed her back toward the harbor. He would have loved to stay out until sunset, but he needed to get his supplies on board and positioned.

"That felt good. Thanks for coming out with me," Ian said quietly as the Whistling Nanny entered the harbor under sail and approached the pier.

"Tim sit down and relax. Let me show you how I plan to moor the Nanny at every pier."

Ian brought the Nanny up to the pier and stopped her and then stepped off and tied her up himself. He knew Tim would pass this on to the owner.

"I have never been with anyone that has handled the Whistling Nanny with such ease and control," Tim said as helped place the deck ramp.

Ian smiled and thanked Tim for the compliment and told him to let the owner know that the Whistling Nanny has a lover as her captain.

On the way back to the office, Ian looked for the security cameras along the pier. There were none but there was one on top of the office building that scanned the entire dock area and one that scanned the parking area.

Ian was pleased that the level of security was rather low. He would be able to lower the water scooter off the stern of the Whistling Nanny and be shielded from the cameras.

"Are there many people who sleep on their boats here at the marina," Ian asked as he looked around at the various boats that were tied up.

"Once in a while some folks come in and are passing through and request overnight type of docking. We put them out there on the far dock. You can see the dock is currently empty. We have an occasional request by those docked here permanently but most of the owners are upscale and prefer their own homes to their boats," Tim replied.

"If you want to stay on board the Whistling Nanny that is Ok," Tim continued.

"Yes, I would like to load my stuff on onboard and then spend time getting everything prepared for sailing," Ian replied.

Ian followed Tim into the office where he signed the papers acknowledging the good condition of the Nanny.

He inspected the boxes being held in storage and arranged for them to be delivered to the ketch.

"Thanks for taking me out for the sea trial," Tim commented as they shook hands.

The sun was now low in the sky as Ian walked back toward the Nanny. He put in a call to his deck hand Ted and to the food service that held the order for the food needed on the trip. Neither party answered and Ian left a message for each.

Ian wanted to have Ted come on board in a day and he wanted the food delivered the day after that. He wanted Ted to store the food so he could manage how it was used.

Ian sat on deck and enjoyed watching the sunset in the west. He felt relaxed for the first time in several weeks. The smell of the ocean and the more distant sound of the waves seemed to soothe him.

Just as the sun went down, Ian heard a request to come on board. Two young men in shorts and sandals, with their hats on backwards were holding two dollies loaded with boxes.

Ian acknowledged them and gave them permission to board. He had them place the boxes in the kitchen area.

The young men made several trips. Their last trip consisted of rolling a large wooden crate that held the water scooter.

"What is in this box. It weighs a ton," one of them asked.

"It's an underwater scooter," Ian replied truthfully. He was not concerned about their idle curiosity.

Ian tipped them well for their service.

After they had left, Ian went about putting away the supplies that had been brought on board. He went out to the Nissan and unloaded the supplies he had brought with him.

The dock area was still and quiet. Ian found the light switch for the lamp posts that lit the area around the Nanny and turned off the lights. He walked up to the dock and ensured the gate was locked.

The lights of the coffee house and the restaurants across the harbor reflected off the dark water. The harbor area had the mysterious look and feeling of a place waiting for some exotic event to occur.

Ian decided on checking out the view from restaurant and bar location and walked up the slight hill. Once there he looked back to where the Nanny was docked.

He felt relieved to see that the Nanny was barely visible. He could relax when he lowered the scooter over the side. It would be almost impossible for anyone to see what he was doing.

Ian walked back to the boat. It took him most of the next hour to remove the scooter from the box.

His team had designed the scooter to mount under the hull behind the keel on two suction mounted hooks.

The V shaped hangers with radio-controlled suction cups at the ends went on like an octopus's suction cup grabbing its prey. Ian tried to pull them loose.

Once satisfied with their holding power, Ian lowered the water scooter down into the water and maneuvered it over to the hangers and secured it. It locked easily and solidly into place. The scooter was now part of the Whistling Nanny.

He mentally complemented his support team for doing a good job.

Ian still had a substantial amount of C4 to deal with. He had left this in the SUV until he was ready to put it into a bullet shaped, waterproof container that attached to the scooter below the hull.

The only trace would be in the SUV. He made sure any trace on his body or clothes were removed.

Ian was just settling down with a cup of ginger tea when he got a call from Ted. They agreed to meet for breakfast at the near-by Bagel shop.

After breakfast they would take the Whistling Nanny for a trial run.

Ian felt good about the pieces of this next phase coming together. He needed to make sure the submersible would ride smoothly and be unnoticeable as the Nanny sailed.

Ted had come highly recommended for his sailing skills and evidently, he cleared the support team's review of his background because they cleared him.

Ian needed to spend a couple of hours making sure Ted was the person to spend the next month with and to learn how well they would work together. He hoped they would get along well.

Ian was up by six the next morning. He mentally went over the entire upcoming trip. He had three more problem solutions ahead of him. Each "*problem*" required a different approach.

The approach to the Tijuana cartel had been the most difficulty for Ian. Since it was down the Baja peninsula in Ensanada an approach from the ocean seemed best.

The Whistling Nanny was a key part of a rather elaborate cover for getting in and out of Ensanada.

The other part of the plan was the fact that he was hosting two couples from Iowa that he had specifically recruited. As part of a dream vacation offer, they had agreed to be his crew for four weeks.

Ian had made the cost very attractive for them under the pretext that they would be part of the Whistling Nanny's crew. He needed them as cover for his cruising into the areas he was going.

Though Ian felt a little guilty about the subterfuge, he knew he would indeed give them an experience that they would talk about for many years to come.

Ian came out of his contemplation and walked up for his Bagel breakfast.

Ian was not overly impressed with the place, but he was focused on meeting Ted. A multi-grained toasted onion bagel with cream cheese and a good cup coffee was all he needed.

The young lady behind the counter was polite and quickly filled his order.

A slender, tall well-tanned, younger man wearing a red sports shirt, black shorts and sandals entered a few moments later. He stopped looked around and walked straight toward Ian.

"Captain Bitterly," he said as he extended his hand.

"Ted, Good morning, call me Matt," Ian replied as they shook hands.

Ian had an immediate good impression.

Ian pointed out of the window to where the Whistling Nanny was moored. In daylight she was a grand sight. The biggest boat in the basin. Her sleek outline spoke of speed and adventure.

"That is a beautiful sight. This is the first time I will crew on this particular boat, but I have had similar experiences on boats not quite as fancy," Ted replied.

"Once you get your stuff on board we will cast off. You are going to have to suffer the overhead bed in the main deck area. It is probably the most convenient location though it will be the one in the middle of the action," Ian advised.

"I am parked in front of the rental office. Is there a place I can leave my car where it will not be towed away," Ted asked?

"I have the same problem. Let's go ask Tim the rental manager about parking and then we can take the Nanny out for a trial run," Ian said as he paid the bill and stood up.

Ian led the way into the rental office to find out where to leave their cars.

Tim suggested that the Platinum long-term parking service would be the best place to leave the cars.

Ian decided to get the cars taken care of first. His car would at a later date be taken care of by his support team. He would never return to the parking lot.

It only took a few minutes to drive up, park and then return by cab.

From Ted's reaction as they boarded the Whistling Nanny, Ian knew that this was the first time he had crewed on a true luxury vessel.

"She is gorgeous," Ted commented as he walked around inspecting and taking a measure of the boat.

"Are you ready to take her out for a trial run," Ian asked as he prepared to cast off.

"Sure, what do you want me to do?" Ted asked.

This time Ian sailed the Nanny out of the harbor area. Once out he had Ted take the helm. Ian sat back, relaxed, and observed how Ted sailed. It was clear to Ian that Ted was indeed capable.

Ian and Ted were back at the pier by noon. He was expecting the food delivery truck at one o-clock. He was pleased with how Ted had performed and how skilled he was at handling the Nanny. He may not have sailed on a top end vessel like the Nanny, but he was skilled in sailing.

"We seem to work well together, and you certainly are qualified on this Bavarian model," Ian said after putting Tim through all the variations of handling the yacht that he could think of.

Ian was just as pleased at how well the two of them got along. This was as important to him as how well Ted performed.

Ian guided the two bringing on the food and Ted put it way in the locations he desired it to go.

Afterwards Ian pulled out the coastal map and showed Ted the route he planned to take along the coast and into the bay of California.

Ted asked about preparing dinner, but Ian suggested having dinner at the Red Fish Fin Inn.

Just before dinner, Ian verified that the remainder of the "crew" was in San Diego. They had checked in at their hotel the evening before. Ian had arranged a day visit for them to Sea World.

The next day, Ian was sitting on deck with Ted enjoying a morning coffee when he saw two couples exit a cab and begin unloading their suitcases.

Ian took in the scene and knew immediately that the four were carrying much more than they would ever need on the cruise. He thought about Lesley's favorite travel agent who said that there were two types of travelers; those who traveled light and those who wished they had traveled light.

"Well, I see two couples up by the head of the pier. Let's go meet them and get them on board."

Ian had thought this cover through carefully and had recruited in only one Iowa location. He had wanted two couples who would be looking for adventure but who knew little about sailing.

He knew that having the couples on board provided a perfect cover. These two young couples were close friends. They had answered Ian's add that promised, "an experience of a lifetime at a price you can afford." The price for the cruise was outrageously low. Ian was subsidizing the true expense.

Once they inquired and agreed to the timing and the cost, Ian pulled the advertising ad. The reason given for the low price was that they would be required to be part of the active crew.

"Hello, you must be Mike and Emily and Jerry and Carla," Ian said as he walked up the pier ramp to where the two couples were standing looking around at the various sailing vessels.

They were staring at the Nanny. The ketch was three times as large as anything currently docked in the basin.

"Is that for us," Emily exclaimed.

"That is the Whistling Nanny and yes that is for the four of you," Ian replied.

Ted and Ian carried several suitcases and each of the couples carried some additional ones.

The two couples came on board and Ian escorted them to their rooms. Their looks of amazement at the luxurious nature of the boat warmed his heart. The cruise was the best buy anyone could ever have hoped to land.

"Do you have all your things on board? Do you have your phones, glasses, wallets, passports," Ian slowly listed all the things he could think might be forgotten?

An image of his Lesley passed through his mind, and he gave an inward chuckle. List checking was her specialty, he was the forgetful one.

"Have you had breakfast yet?"

"We talked about having breakfast, but we were afraid to miss meeting you," Emily volunteered.

It was only seven in the morning. Ian had counted on them having to get up early to get to the dock.

"Let me introduce Ted Nickson, second in command of the Whistling Nanny. Let's see if he can whip up a good breakfast for all of us. He cooks but you all will clean. This morning's limited menu includes eggs any way you like, pancakes, sausage, or bacon or both," Ian rattled off.

"Ted make sure there is enough for the two of us," Ian added.

"So is there an experienced sailor among the lot of you," Ian asked as if he didn't already know the answer.

He had sent them a primer on sailing when they had sent in his earlier questionnaire.

"That's an unfair question since we already gave you the answer," Carla said from her side of the table.

"Ok, fair enough. Have you all studied your sailing primer," Ian asked next?

"We did, and we took two small sailing boats out on the lake to practice," Mike volunteered.

Ted delivered breakfast to Emily and Carla. Each had ordered two eggs and sausage.

"Good for you. That puts you one step closer to becoming a qualified deck hand," Ian replied with a smile.

"Next question, have you selected a motion sickness treatment recommended by your doctors," Ian asked?

"Good," Ian said as he saw them nod yes with their heads.

"Do you each have your passport and tourist Visa for Mexico?" Ian inquired next.

"Please get them out and put them in the waterproof plastic zip lock bag by the radio," Ian instructed and pointed to where the bag was clearly visible.

"Let me see the Tourist Visa please," Ian requested as they got their passports out.

Ted brought the breakfast for Mike and Jerry. The two of them had ordered two over easy eggs, two pancakes and two sausages.

"Ted I'll take what they are having but put my eggs on top of the two pancakes and bring the butter and syrup to the table," Ian requested.

They had all signed a contract as working crew members. This had been Ian's stated reason for the low price for the cruise.

"You all agreed to and signed a contract to crew on this trip. You will learn to sail the Nanny and take assigned watches at the helm. Are you ready for this," Ian asked?

"Sure, but will you train us before you leave us alone," Mike inquired.

"Actually, until you get many, many hours at the helm either Ted or I will be sitting here at the table or out behind you relaxing but on watch with you," Ian replied.

"Each of you will cook one meal a day. My cookbook is available, and I have the ingredients for anything in my cookbook. It is a simple cookbook. If you know better recipes, please feel free to add them. You will be able to prepare steaks, fish, lamb, shrimp, and a variety of other seafood items. Are you ready for your cooking responsibilities," Ian put the question out?

These were foods on the survey they had returned to him as part of their purchase.

"Can we ask for help in preparing our meals. I mean can one of our group help me or Mike," Jerry asked?

"This is not a test. You are all free to do what you want during your time on board. Certainly, help each other in everything," Ian replied.

Ted will do much of the work but each of you will join in to help as needed.

Ian stood up and took the two couples for a tour while Ted got the Nanny ready to sail.

Today each of you will take a turn in each position. Ted will take the Nanny out. After lunch we will stop for a swim around three or so.

Tomorrow we should make Ensenada by early evening.

Dinner tonight will be provided by the person on the list named to cook the evening meal. The entire cooking schedule is posted on the refrigerator.

Ted will help you cook the meals today. You can discuss among yourselves who will do the cooking first.

Any questions," Ian asked as he looked at each of them?

They were all smiles and chattering to each other. It was clear they were going to enjoy themselves.

Ian returned to the table and inspected the passports, their visas and made sure the passports were secured by the radio. He knew the coast guard from either or both the US and Mexico would stop them to check.

The sun was at its zenith before Ian had the two couples oriented, moved in and in general ready to go. He spent extra time getting them familiar with the Nanny and discussing safety out on the high seas.

Finally, Ian declared it was time to cast off. He made each couple cast off one of the mooring lines.

Ted, his red hat on backwards, his feet spread, standing in a relaxed manner with the Nanny's wheel in his left hand was the picture of a modern romantic pirate.

Ian raised a sun cover that went across the stern of the Nanny and sat back in the shade enjoying the smooth motion as the Nanny climbed the long period Pacific Ocean swells at a sixty-degree angle and then went smoothly down the back slope. It was a smooth mesmerizing ride.

Ian watched as Mike and Emily washed and put away the breakfast dishes while Jeremy and Carla looked through the cookbook trying to decide what they would prepare for lunch. By their enthusiastic chatter, it was clear they were immediately enjoying themselves.

A few minutes later the four of them were looking at the navigation chart that Ian had put on the table. Ian had penciled in the route he planned to follow and made some notations about the events he had planned along the trip route. The four were absorbed by where they were going and what they would see.

Ian knew that they would cross the border into Mexico sometime around the noon hour. Of course, at sea, it was impossible to tell one side of the border from the other. The map clearly showed the line separating the two countries. The ocean looked the same on both sides of the border.

Ian saw a ship approaching them from the forward port bow.

"Have you decided on what you are preparing for lunch," Ian inquired?

"Yes, we decided on having hamburgers and hot dogs," Carla replied.

"Get them on the grill. We are about to get company. I will offer them some lunch," Ian said as he pointed to what looked like a small destroyer escort.

He figured it would most likely be the Mexican Coast Guard.

"I believe it is the Mexican Coast Guard coming out to greet us. Take it easy and let me do the talking," Ian instructed.

Ian arranged his sailing permit and the passports. He had Ted lower the mainsail. Then they waited for the Coast Guard to come along side.

Ian had all his paperwork ready when the Mexican Coast Guard hailed them.

"Buen día, es bueno tener a que nos visite. Aquí están todos nuestros pasaportes, visas y documentos de los buques," Ian greeted the coast guard inspector as he came on board.

"This is a vacation cruise for my passengers. I am taking them to see the whales and I will do some underwater filming," Ian continued to explain in Spanish as he showed him his camera equipment.

The Coast Guard officer was cordial, chatted with each of the guests as he checked their passports and tourist visas.

Ian planned to do the filming and send it to his old acquaintance he had from the Elephants and Ivory documentary adventure. He hoped to get some footage that would blow Andrea's mind.

"Would you and your crew care for some American hamburgers or hot dogs," Ian extended his invitation.

Gracias, voy a aceptar perros calientes para todos mis marineros. Hay ocho de nosotros a bordo. Podemos enviarlos a la nave?

"Yes of course. Eight hotdogs to go with ketchup and mustard and of course napkins," Ian replied loud enough for Carla to hear.

Carla responded with a thumbs up.

The officer checked out the paperwork. Briefly looked around. He accepted the bag of hot dogs and wished everyone a good time.

Ian watched the Mexican Coast Guard cruise away.

Let's have lunch, relax, and take time for a swim, Ian declared.

The Mexican Coast guard disappeared over the horizon. They were headed in the same direction as Ian and his crew. Ian was sure they would be moored very close to the Coast Guard base in Ensenada.

Amazing as it seemed, the Tijuana cartel had their headquarters in a warehouse almost directly across the harbor from the base. This was just amazing to Ian. It gave new meaning to hiding in plain sight.

Ian figured some high-ranking Coast Guard officer was getting a healthy bonus to add to his government pay.

Ian had rented dock space for five days. He hoped to be able to approach the cartel's warehouse from the water side. The water approach would be risky, but Ian had more confidence in it than any other.

He had made sure he was arriving at the time of the month that had the darkest, moonless nights. He needed really dark nights to aid him in getting into the warehouse unseen. He was leaving nothing to luck but would take good luck willingly if it came his way. Ian felt luck was always good.

The coast came into view as they sailed almost directly east. The sun was low on the horizon behind them.

Ian had the Nanny within sight of the "Islas de Todos Santos," All Saints Island.

"The islands you see to the starboard has some of the best snorkeling in the world. You will have a great time learning to scuba near those islands," Ian shared.

The sun was just setting as the Nanny docked at the pier.

"Let's plan on a leisurely dinner and then we will spend tomorrow snorkeling and learning to dive. Tonight, we can spend time on instruction and each of you can examine your scuba tanks," Ian suggested.

This would give Ian a chance to examine the harbor and get a firsthand look at what he faced.

Ian pointed out the box shaped coast on the navigation map. The harbor area was on the Northeast corner of the box. This was where the cruise ships came in. It was the largest of three harbors in the Ensenada area.

When they came in, they immediately saw a cruise ship dominating the harbor. As they came in, Emily pointed to her right where the coast guard boat that had checked them out. It was moored next to a destroyer that made the coast guard boat look small.

Ian was at the helm taking the Nanny to the berth he had rented for the next week. He had called ahead to the Cruise Port office, and he could see someone standing at the end of the pier that he had rented.

The Nanny was the largest sailing vessel in the dock area. There was one other ketch almost the same size at the end of the next dock.

This part of the harbor held about a hundred ocean going power boats and a few sailing vessels. The cruise ship was docked in the large part of the harbor. It was directly in front of them and dominated the view to the west. It was the largest structure in the Ensanada area.

Ian brought the Nanny to a smooth stop and his "crew" tied her forward and aft mooring lines the way they had practiced it. The side bumpers had been deployed just prior to getting next to the pier.

"Great job," Ian called out as he cut the engine.

Ian called the crew together.

I just called my local tour guide, and she is ready to take you all out for the evening. You get two evenings out here in Ensanada as part of the tour package. This includes all you can eat and drink.

Do you want to skip dinner on board and go out into Ensenada early or would you rather eat on board?

It was no surprise to Ian that the unanimous answer was to go out.

He had hoped that would be the answer.

Ian assigned Ted to go with them. He called the local guide and asked her to meet the group at the entrance to the dock area.

Ian let everyone know he was going to stay on board.

Once they were on their way, Ian lowered the battery for the submersible over the side. He put on his scuba gear and slipped quietly into the water. He was going to transit the harbor in the dark using the GPS on his phone. This was a first for him.

He hoped to miss the giant tour ship.

The water in the harbor was clear. Since it was a very dark night it really did not matter. All Ian could see were the lights of the harbor.

Ian's eyes were on the screen of his phone located in a recessed shielded holder on the submersible. Ian marveled at the fact that he was crossing the harbor in pitch black darkness following a picture on his phone.

He had calculated the distance across the harbor at almost four nautical miles. At top speed he reached his destination in a little over thirty minutes.

Ian surfaced briefly to get a visual of the area and to make sure he was in the proximity of the right warehouse. He then dropped an anchor and secured his supply of C4 and the monitoring equipment to the floor of the harbor.

His return trip was significantly faster but in total the trip consumed a little over an hour.

Ian reattached the submersible to the hooks just behind the keel. Once on deck Ian stored his wetsuit and recharged his scuba tank.

He then took a leisurely shower and went to bed.

8 Tijuana Cartel

Ian woke slowly up. It was two in the morning. The whispering chatter and quiet laughter let him know that the "crew" had returned from their evening out. He was sure he would have the early morning to himself.

Ian was up at six and by six thirty he was standing at the helm with a cup of coffee guiding the Nanny out of the Harbor. He had not bothered to get anyone up.

Ahead Ian had just sighted the All-Saints Islands when Ted came up the steps and back to the helm with his cup of coffee.

"You should have awakened me," Ted said groggily.

"I would have worried about you falling overboard," Ian joked.

"How was the evening outing," Ian inquired?

Ted replied that he had a good time and that the rest of the crew had a wonderful time.

Ian brought the sail down and let the Nanny coast down slowly. Then he dropped anchor. The northern island was about a thousand yards away and the Nanny was just shy of the coral reef that would provide good snorkeling and good scuba diving.

The Nanny, the sleeping crew are all yours Ian declared. I am going to prepare some breakfast and then relax out here until everyone is up and ready for the day.

About an hour later the two couples had awakened and were in the galley.

"After you have had breakfast, we will begin with some snorkeling. Once you have had a chance to see it from on top, Ted will be your diving guide below," Ian said as he finished his breakfast and went back on deck and sat under the awning.

The day went by slowly for Ian. He got everyone out either snorkeling or diving. Ted guided the diving while Ian worked with the snorkelers.

Ian took his waterproof laminated fish observation charts with all the tropical and commercial fishes out with him. He had the four snorkelers check off each specific type of fish as it was observed. Everything went smoothly until several sand sharks swam by. The four clustered around Ian as if he would provide a shield.

Ian had his professional camera in the water with him and took a series of pictures. He had more than a dozen pictures of the commercial fish and hundreds of pictures of tropical fish from barely visible in size up to those that were several feet long.

He was able to capture some great pictures of the sharks.

Ian called everyone on board for a late lunch and announced that the group had an evening dinner reservation at the Santo Thomas Winery. They would enjoy a tour and then a late dinner. Afterwards they could once again enjoy the night life.

He then let them know about their Saturday schedule for a tour to La Bufadora and on their return they would stop by the open-air market for some souvenir shopping.

"This is great. I was a doubter when we signed the contract for this vacation trip, but it has already exceeded my expectations," Mike commented.

Ian looked calmly back at the group with a smile and thought, "You are right buddy. If it is too good to be true it probably is not true." You are lucky that my subterfuge did not cost you.

It was clear the two couples were eager to party.

After the snorkeling and the diving there was still a good part of the afternoon left.

"It's time for some sailing lessons. Stand around me. Emily stand at the helm you get the privilege of getting the first lesson," Ian said as he stepped away from the wheel.

"Let's up anchor and get underway," he continued.

The lessons went on into late afternoon and everyone got their turn at the wheel.

"We all want to thank you for this experience," Carla said as Ian brought the Nanny up to the pier.

"Ted says his tip jar is by the sink," Ian joked with her.

"Kids, he is joking. I don't have a tip jar but if you want my bank account number, I will give it to you," Ted joined in on the banter.

Ian had already made sure Ted got top pay for this trip and had told him he got twenty percent more as a tip for putting up with him.

"Well, I see your guide for the evening is arriving. Go get ready and then hit the town," Ian instructed as he put out the gang way and went ashore to meet with the tour guide.

"Mi nombre es Mateo. Gracias por venir. Por favor, dar a estos jóvenes gringos una buena noche en la ciudad y disfrutar también," Ian greeted the tour guide and told her to show the group a good time and to enjoy herself as well.

"I am Andrea. And thank you for being so generous," Andrea replied as Ian led her on board.

It took another hour for everyone to be ready. Andrea enjoyed a drink and commented on how nice the boat looked.

The sun had set, and the night was quickly getting dark. This seemed to be a perfect night for what Ian had in his plans.

Once again Ian sent Ted with the rest of the crew. It was clear that Ted was bonding well with the other four.

Ian was planning to utilize the evening to get into the cartel warehouse and put everything into place.

The crew left the Nanny as the final light of the day died. Ian packed a waterproof bag with all the listening devices, timers, and fuses. He then lowered everything into the water and in his scuba gear he went under the Nanny and unhooked the scooter.

The clear screen of his I phone shining up from its shielded holder and his depth reading were the only visible things Ian could see. The cruise ship had departed so Ian was able to shave off a couple of minutes transit time.

Ian went across as fast as he could. He wanted to be in and out as quickly as possible. He hoped that lady luck was on his side this evening.

If possible, he planned to make an appearance and mingle with the rest of the crew. This would seal his alibi if he were to need one.

Ian hoped the Mexican Navy did not have any sophisticated listening or sonar equipment in use in the harbor. The low almost unnoticeable hum and vibration of the submersible made him nervous, but the crossing was uneventful.

Ian located the bag with the C4 explosives. He attached everything to the submersible and slowly approached the pier.

The large warehouse building had external guard towers looking out over the harbor, but it appeared they would not be able to see below the edge of the pier. Ian went under the pier as far as possible. The piers had maintenance hatches every few hundred feet. Ian anchored his load to a piling and went about finding a hatch. He was looking for a hatch that was close to one of the main doors from the warehouse out to the pier.

Ian looked through the slit of the slightly lifted hatch. The towers had a clear view of the entire pier surface.

"Good for them bad for me," Ian thought as he lowered the hatch.

At the second hatch, Ian located a door almost next to it. Getting the explosives and other equipment into the warehouse would be a challenge but doable from this location. He moved all the gear to the top rung of the ladder.

Ian would need to act swiftly when the guards were looking in some other direction.

He hoped they had been guarding the pier for so long that they were bored stiff by the lack of any action.

Ian spent at least twenty minutes getting to know the pattern of the guards. It appeared to him that these guards had done this for many nights and days. They spent a great deal of time out of sight, probably sitting and talking to each other.

It appeared that the tower lights were fixed but Ian was sure there would be movable ones that could be manually manipulated. There was no moon, so it would be as dark as it ever got in these parts.

His small mirror provided a means to monitor the two towers. Ian opened the hatch completely. He hoped it would not be noticed.

He moved immediately to the door. As he expected it was locked. He picked the lock as quickly as he could. He was swearing under his breath the entire time.

Ian found the alarm contacts and put a jumper across them before opening the door. Then he opened door only wide enough to squeeze in.

No alarm! He immediately let out his breath.

Ian stood completely still. He was looking at a warehouse full of pallets stacked on high rise racks. He scanned the ceiling for cameras and made note of the lighting. He located three cameras but was sure there would be others. The first one that would need to me neutralized was the one directly above his head.

Ian carefully turned the cameras so there would be a clear lane for him to get to the warehouse office area.

He moved slowly. He was looking for motion sensors. At this point any alarm would end his attempt to set up the trap he had in mind.

It was a relief to learn there were no internal guards. A human guard always increased the level of complexity. He would still maintain his vigil since one of the guards from the tower might make an hourly run. If that were the case Ian would need to be out of the warehouse in the next thirty minutes.

Ian thanked the gods that the door to the warehouse opened inward since this decreased the chance of detection as he brought in his gear.

Slowly and carefully, Ian moved his equipment into the warehouse. He gave a sigh of relief once he got all his material in.

He calculated it was now almost a half an hour into the work. He needed about fifteen minutes to conceal the explosive charges and then another fifteen minutes to get back out of the warehouse. He truly hoped the guards were lax about any rounds they might make.

There were two main meeting rooms and one grand office. Ian selected the positions for the various charges.

He also carefully placed and concealed the listening devices.

He had brought along a variety of camouflage material to cover the various charges. He covered the charge under the main desk with a cloth similar to the color of the wood under the desk. It was virtually invisible.

Ian admired his work and thought that perhaps he should have been an interior decorator.

All the explosives were surface mounted with either cone or starfish shaped deflectors. Each charge also contained a handful of steel fragments.

There would be carnage in every one of these rooms when the charges went off. However, Ian's intent was to keep the explosions contained.

The explosive charges were designed to be focused with just enough power to take out the target in its vicinity. He was hoping to minimize any collateral deaths of the office workers.

Ian was counting on his listening devices to locate the intended targets. He finalized the placement of the listening devices carefully around the rooms and office area.

Ian would have loved to install some video cameras to see his targets, but this was beyond what he was able to do while keeping the risk of discovery down.

Ian planned to periodically energize the listening system and then de-energized while he was waiting. He hoped this approach would ensure that the equipment would not be found.

For the next several days, he planned to be in and out of the harbor listening.

Finally done, Ian returned to the exit door. He held an empty waterproof duffel bag. He was ready to return to the ketch.

Getting back out of the building was as dangerous as getting in. Getting caught leaving would be the ultimate failure. A sense of relief went through Ian as he closed the hatch on the dock floor above him.

He waited several minutes to make sure he had not been discovered.

Ian got quietly into the water and bundled up the underwater float.

The trip back was anticlimactic and much faster than the trip over.

After securing the submersible and leaving his wetsuit and all his clothes with the scooter, completely nude Ian got on board the Nanny and immediately took a long hot shower. He did not want any C4 residue to be detected.

It was too late to join the rest of the crew. Ian's two couples could be heard laughing and singing as they came back from their night out. They found him sitting on deck and drinking a Negra Modelo.

Ian suggested a night cap that they all accepted. Ted went about getting the beers or wine.

They all opted for a Corona with a lime and were soon seated around Ian chattering away.

They had loved the trip to the winery and the dinner there and thanked Ian for the arrangement.

They had loved the Mariachi players and the general friendliness of the Mexican people. Just before going to bed, they asked about the coming two days of scuba, snorkeling and sailing.

"We will do a lot more of each in the next few days and will stop only when you say uncle. Don't forget that you will go to the blowhole La Bufadora and the market tomorrow. I will join you on that excursion. Sunday it will be all sunshine, swimming, and sailing" Ian reminded them.

Ian said goodnight to Ted and went into his room. He was looking forward to a good night's sleep. This time he would not be bruised and battered. He would just remain anxious.

The next day, Ian relaxed and took in the ride south on highway 1 and then across on highway 23 along the southern coast of All Saints Bay. The tour van turned south and cross the peninsula to get to the town of La Bufadora. The town had grown only because of tourism. It was little more than one or two buildings deep on either side of the road that led to the viewing area.

This was Ian's first time to see the blow hole. The van stopped and the six of them walked the rest of the way toward the viewing area.

Andrea, their guide, led them on a walk that took them to the highest lookout point above the blow hole. Below them they could see a hoard of tourists. They were the only ones on their higher level. The view was better than the tourist viewing area.

After watching the event for the third time, Ian was ready for lunch and the trip back to the market.

Periodically, Ian activated the listening devices in the warehouse. All was silent as he expected it to be for the weekend.

The van took them to the market where Ian strolled casually through observing the tourists and the shop keepers. Everyone was engaged in their particular shopping endeavor. He did some looking but had no interest in buying anything.

That evening the crew once again went out for dinner and drinks.

Sunday morning Ian sailed out to the north tip of the Banda Peninsula. Once there he gave a choice to his guests to go on a scuba excursion led by Ted or to snorkel with him.

Mike and Emily preferred to snorkel. Emily could not get over her phobia about breathing through her scuba mouthpiece.

Jerry and Carla on the other hand always maxed out their scuba time.

The morning passed quickly and sailing lessons filled the afternoon. Ian enjoyed letting the Nanny loose and augmenting the main sail with the head sail to put the Nanny to full speed.

Late in the afternoon, Ian brought the Nanny back to the dock.

This was an evening that was free for everyone to do as they pleased. Ian had decided to relax on the Nanny and was surprised when the rest of the crew joined him and asked if he would join them playing one of the games they had requested. It turned out to be a great evening where everyone was chatting, laughing, and sharing what a wonderful time they all were enjoying.

Monday morning the activity in the warehouse came to life. There was activity in the main office and the small meeting area. Ian had on what appeared to be an i-pod and earplugs as he sailed out of the harbor. This allowed him to monitor the warehouse as he played cruise captain.

Ian delayed the departure by slowly moving over to where he could get the boat fueled up.

"I'm making a small change in our plans. We will fuel up and then sail on down the coast. This will get us into the bay of California sooner. We can continue our scuba and snorkeling activities each afternoon and then do some more once we get into the bay. You will all take turns sailing the Nanny on the way there," Ian informed the group.

After fueling, he sailed out of the harbor about eleven in the morning.

Just before lunch the main warehouse meeting area became a beehive of activity. Ian was having a hard time keeping up with what was transpiring. A major cartel business meeting was getting ready to take place.

The conversation in the office was what consignments went to which location and who was going to be responsible to make sure they made it to their destinations and collected the money.

Someone had been lax in their performance. There was some sort of infringement by the Pacific Cartel and someone in the Mexican Navy wanted more money.

These conversations eased Ian's conscience about the upcoming event.

There seemed to be two groups working different issues. Both were high intensity discussions and arguments. There seemed to be a great degree of tension and hostility.

Ian decided it would be best to set off the charges while the two groups were separated. This would be the most devastating.

The Whistling Nanny was just beyond the mouth of the harbor when Ian activated the explosives.

What followed was not what he had expected.

The entire waterfront section of the warehouse blew out. It was followed by large flames and flying debris. Even on the Nanny the roar was deafening.

Ian knew immediately that the warehouse must have housed a lot of explosives of its own. What he had planted would never have caused the explosion that had just occurred.

So far almost every explosive he had set was augmented by the explosives possessed by the cartels.

"What in the world was that" Emily asked.

"I guess some sort of industrial explosion," Ian replied as the harbor fire department boats raced toward the warehouse.

Ted was at the helm taking the Nanny out, so Ian stood with the other four and watched the scene.

It was clear to Ian that everyone in the warehouse would be dead. Once again, the collateral damage was much greater than Ian had planned.

Ian turned and looked out to sea.

He felt bad about the lowly workers in the office area. They most probably had mediocre jobs and mediocre pay and were only trying to make a living.

The Nanny caught the wind and sailed smoothly out. About an hour later the Nanny rounded the Banda Peninsula and headed down the coast toward the tip of the California Peninsula.

An hour later, Carla pointed aft at what appeared to be the Mexican Coast Guard Vessel. It seemed to be closing the distance between them.

Ian instructed Mike to swing to starboard and lower the main to two thirds mast. The Nanny slowed down.

Ian watched as the Coast Guard adjusted their course to intercept them.

Ian walked over to where he had stored the controls to the submersible hangers and pushed the button to release and drop the submersible. He hated to lose it, but he figured this time there would be a more thorough inspection. He could not afford to have the submersible be found.

Shortly afterwards the Nanny was hailed and ordered to stop. Jeremy was on the helm, and it was clear he was very nervous.

Ian told everyone to relax and that he would do the talking.

It was the same boat that had stopped them a few days before. He saw that a diver was getting into the dingy that was going to cross over to the Nanny. The same officer that had come on board before was also on the boat, there was also another sailor with a dog.

Since the Baja coastline was in view, Ian knew that the Nanny was still in Mexican waters. He told the crew to relax and that he would handle everything.

"It is good to see you again but what brings you out," Ian asked in his best Spanish?

A major explosion occurred in the harbor this morning, you are the only boat that is leaving the area. We have been sent out to inspect your boat and to clear you of having anything to do with the incident, the officer replied as he came on board.

We heard and saw much of what happened. We gave you our itinerary when we last met, and we are on our way to the Gulf of California, Ian replied.

The handler and the dog came onboard at the same time.

"Do you mind if the dog examines the inside of the boat, and my diver examines the hull of your boat.

"Crew, it looks like this could take a few moments. Let's stop for lunch.

Should we prepare enough for your crew? I think you plan your timing so that you can have a good lunch, Ian joked with the inspector.

It was clear the inspector was feeling a little embarrassed. The diver in the water came back aboard the Nanny and removed his scuba gear.

He explained there was nothing on the hull.

This time the inspector accepted twelve hamburgers and an equal number of Cokes.

Gracious, and accept my apology for having interrupted your sailing trip," the inspector said as he and his crew got into their dingy and went back toward their boat.

"No es nada, y que son bienvenidos en cualquier momento," Ian replied.

Ian informed the crew that he wanted to make it to the Cedros Island where they would anchor off the San Benito Island.

I am going to take a nap; your job is to take your turns at the helm. Keep us on course and get us to our anchor point before the sun sets. Ian informed his vacationing crew.

Ted indicated he would stay on duty.

Ian had rented a dock space at Cabo San Lucas. He was surprised that everything was going on schedule. He had been concerned about being stopped by the coast guard and was gratified that they had found nothing and had not made him return with them to the harbor. He had sacrificed his submersible but that was a small cost as compared to getting caught with it.

Ian had again arranged for an evening out for his four vacationing crew members. He joined them for dinner and then sent them off with Ted to experience the night life. Once again, they had a local tour guide to accompany them.

Ian looked at the map on the table. Cabo San Lucas was at the southern tip of the Baja Peninsula. The Pacific Cartel was his next target. They were located just outside of Culiacan.

9 Baha Transit

He would have a few days of rest and relaxation before working on the next solution.

The Gulf was a known location for whales and a host of other sea life. Ian hoped to enjoy this brief respite in between his more odious actions. Ian put his pencil on the map and made an asterisk at a point in the middle of the Gulf just across form the coastal city of La Reforma located on the eastern side.

Ian poured himself a cup of coffee and walked out on deck. He felt good about the four vacationing crew members. They were becoming a good crew and seemed to be enjoying every moment. Jeremy was stretching the Nanny and letting her run as fast as he could get her. He had become the best sailor.

The Nanny was slicing smoothly through the water as if it were sliding through soft butter.

Everyone else except Emily who was cleaning up from breakfast was sitting around enjoying the breeze blowing back their hair and the morning sun warming their souls.

The appearance of all of them had darkened or in Jeremy's case reddened from their time at sea. They would return home as totally new people. They would not only look good; they would be more confident and surer of themselves.

Ian walked up to the bow to look ahead.

He almost immediately spotted a large manta ray traveling in the same direction as the Nanny.

He called out to Jeremy to sail along in parallel to and stay with the manta. Ian went below and brought out his camera equipment and set it up and began filming.

With Ted's help Jeremy brought the Nanny slowly toward the manta.

Ian wanted to get as close to the manta as possible. Looking through his camera, Ian gave Jeremy navigation instructions that slowly brought the Nanny almost within reach.

The entire crew was now standing around him talking about the size and graceful beauty of the giant manta.

Ian continued filming until the manta turned and went down out of sight.

Ian was pleased with the film he had.

For the rest of the day and well into the evening Ian kept himself occupied editing the footage of the manta. He also integrated his earlier filming and picture taking. He was pleased with the results.

The next morning, Ian was enjoying a first cup of coffee when Ted let him know that they were almost at the point on the map where there was an asterisk and nothing more.

Ian had picked the northern most point to which he intended to sail. Here he planned to spend a day or two and then sail to La Reforma where he would leave the Nanny.

The asterisk was some thirty miles offshore from the eastern side of the Gulf and the water depth was sixty feet. This would allow the Nanny to drop anchor. Ian hoped to see some of the abundant and diverse sea life that had their home in this area.

Ian looked around three hundred and sixty degrees and saw only water. The sky was the light clear blue that always made him think of the paint he painted the baby room for the birth of his first son. In contrast the sea around him was a blue that seemed dark but when he looked down it was clear, and it seemed he could see the bottom.

"Drop the sails. Let the Nanny drift to a stop and check the depth and drop anchor if we are at about sixty feet," was Ian's reply.

Breakfast was being prepared by Jeffery. Ian was having his favorite breakfast of two pancakes with two over easy eggs on top and three sausages. He lifted the pancake and with his knife put in a slice of butter and then poured on a healthy helping of maple syrup. He then did the same on top.

Emily commented that she had never seen anyone eat pancakes in quite this manner and that it would kill him.

Ian admitted that he would try to keep that from happening. He figured his death would come from something much more direct and sinister.

Ian then shared the edited shots of the giant manta ray. He had merged in some footage from pictures he had taken of the fish he had taken during their earlier scuba and snorkeling sessions. The combination created a totally different world.

Carla and Mike both commented that they would never have believed they were seeing what they knew they had personally seen and that they would love to have a copy.

Ian shared his plan to let the Nanny stay anchored for a day or two and take in what the Gulf had to offer. He planned to spend time in the water around the Nanny with his underwater camera in hopes of getting some additional good footage.

He let them know that anyone that was interested could hang out with him.

Everyone wanted to go into the water. Ted volunteered to stay on the Nanny. Everyone went about getting their gear in order and then getting into their wetsuits.

Ian arranged his gear on deck. His camera was a small newly released professional underwater camera about the size of a romance paperback book. He had selected it on the recommendation of an underwater photographer friend that had lauded the quality of the pictures and the ease of handling the camera.

It was a great recommendation, but it really was the small size that would be more manageable in the water that had connected with Ian.

Ian led the way by dropping backward off the back platform.

He signaled the group to gather together. He took his shots from below them. The white hull of the Nanny could be seen clearly above them.

Almost immediately Ian spotted and began filming a curious Pacific Hawk Bill sea turtle, its black scale sections centered with orange fading to yellow patches and its white and black patched front legs swam directly toward them. It came within twenty feet and went down to a deeper level.

Ian turned to the other divers capturing their thumbs up gestures. Emily began to gesture with her finger to something behind him.

Ian had a momentary start but relaxed when he realized he was looking at another giant manta ray. Its head on approach gave him a great shot of the mouth bracketed on each side by two paddle like protrusions. A white sucker fish had attached itself to the top right side. The pair made their approach and like the turtle veered off and went by the group at a close but not a threatening distance.

Their presence indicated that the area they were in was active. Ian hoped the display of sea life would keep up.

Ian decided it was a good time to take a break. He signaled the group to go up.

"This is the life. I am glad we agreed to this vacation," Jeffery said as he relaxed in the sun and drank Pellegrino with some freshly squeezed lime.

"Look out there, I see a whale, Emily called from her seat on the bow.

Ian looked and realized there were three whales. They provided a sense of wonder and awe.

He acted immediately and got everyone into the water. Everyone was eager to see the whales up close.

A mother humpback whale approached the group. Her young calf was swimming as if hugging her side and a second young whale just slightly smaller than the mother swam a little behind but provided a shield for the calf.

Ian moved some distance away from the others so he could get them and the whale in the same picture. He captured some great shots that had the group and the whales and one with the hull of the Nanny behind the entire setting.

Then the mother came directly at Ian. To Ian it looked as if she would hit him but at the last moment she went sliding by to his left.

Ian instinctively put his left arm over the top fin and caught a ride with the mother. She seemed not to notice. It took all his strength to hold on and swing his legs over her back as if she was a horse. He positioned himself in a sitting position but holding on for everything he was worth.

Ian was getting some really great close ups of the young baby whale. The mother made a large circle around the four swimmers.

Ian released his hold as it appeared the whale trio was going to leave the area. He swam back toward the group in the water.

Ian was going to signal getting back on to the Nanny when he spotted a pod of killer whales coming toward them. He figured they were following the mother whale with her baby.

Ian once again swam away from the group so he could capture them with the approaching killer whales. Once again, the camera seemed to attract the attention. To Ian, it seemed they were coming straight at him. He took in a deep breath and slowly released it in a continuous stream of bubbles.

He got his nerves under control.

The lead killer whale came right toward him. Ian threw one leg up and over him and mounted him facing backwards with the top fin between his legs. He had his chest up against the top fin.

Ian kept the camera going as each of the accompanying killers took a turn coming up to him as if to get a closer look or a better picture pose. None of them seemed aggressive. Their path followed the same one taken by the mother whale and her young. They too made a circle around the four in the water.

Ian figured the killer whales were probably following some scent that remained in the water. He hoped that the mother whale and her young would outwit this group of hunters.

As the lead killer whale finished its circle one of the followers came up and nudged Ian from his seat.

He was happy that he had not been on their lunch menu.

Ian knew that he had taken some of the best underwater sea life footage that had ever been captured. He knew who he was going to grace with the footage.

This time he gave the signal for everyone to go up. He had used almost all of his air.

"I can't believe what you did out there. You must be crazy," Jerry said as everyone got back on board. The other three agreed.

"I thought the whale was going to take you out. Each time the killer whales came at you, I thought the game was over.," Emily added.

"I just wanted to get out of the water and not be eaten," Carla said as she dried herself off.

"Well yes, I have been called crazy before. It seems animals relate well to me and understand I mean them no harm," Ian replied with a smile.

Ian took the memory chip from the camera and immediately created several backups of the original footage.

He let everyone know he was going to process the pictures he had taken. He worked rapidly on a first cut edit to share with the folks on the Nanny.

Ian wondered what Andria Miller of his Elephants and Ivory adventure would think when she got this footage in her mail. Ian would bequeath it to her since he personally would never be able to put this out publicly.

Ian wondered if the animals sensed his internal calm or somehow knew of his secret profession. Ian had capture elephants, lions, and other fierce animals up close and personal, and none had ever threatened him. Ian admitted to having played subservient to the giant silver back gorilla, but he had never felt threatened. He loved the interactions he had experienced with the wild animals.

The raw film footage was a big hit on the Nanny. It was several hours long and was highlighted by the two rides. However, it also had footage of the twenty-foot giant manta ray and a brief shot of the smaller six-foot reef manta.

A lone Leather Back Sea turtle and a Pacific Hawkbill turtle made cameo appearances.

Close ups of a variety of fish rounded out the cast.

"Unbelievable," was the phrase that kept coming up as the couples watched the raw film.

"I was out there with you, and I didn't see half of what you caught on camera," Jerry commented.

"This is like watching some of those National Geographic nature films. Let's see it again," Carla added.

Ian wished he could spend his time doing nature films. Then he amended his thought since he realized he was not being totally honest with himself. He could do whatever he wanted, and he realized he was doing exactly that.

Many opportunities to do something less dangerous had presented themselves over the years. He had never taken those off ramps.

There was just something about pitting himself against the bad guys that trumped every other thing he had ever thought of doing.

Ian knew it was time for him to take action on the next cartel.

He had a smile on his face as he told Ted that he was promoting him to the status of Captain.

Ted said sure thing, but when Ian went on to explain that he had officially submitted papers to that effect with the State of California Ted had tears in his eyes. Ian told him the official paperwork should be in his mailbox by the time he returned the Nanny to its port.

He also let Ted know that he was going to depart when they got into port.

Ted was overwhelmed. Ian knew that achieving the level of Captain was one of Ted's personal goals. Ted was excited about finishing the trip as captain and assured Ian that the Nanny and its crew would safely return to California.

The next morning at breakfast, Ian informed the rest of the Nanny's crew that there was a personal emergency and that he would be leaving them at the next port. He let them know that Ted had officially been promoted to captain. The next celebration would be to celebrate Ted's accomplishment.

He listened politely to the praise of the four "vacationing crew members" and then suggested that they all have dinner and a beer together once they docked in La Reforma.

The Nanny was at the La Reforma dock by late afternoon.

The evening out was on Ian. He joined everyone for dinner and a few drinks. Then he said his goodbyes and promised them that he would keep in touch. He would but they would never know his real identity.

He then walked down the street to where an old pickup was parked. It was one of the support items Ian had requested from his invisible and remote team of helpers.

10 The Sinaloa Cartel

*I*an looked at the wind worn grey paint of the old pickup. It passed for an old local pickup that a subsistence farmer would be driving. The condition of the tires indicated it was in good shape.

He put the few possessions he was carrying with him in the bed of the truck. He tried the combination lock on the side of what appeared to be a beat-up metal box. He looked inside and counted the bundles of explosives, took note that the timers and remote detonation equipment were all in the box. Satisfied that he had what was needed, Ian closed the box.

He prepared to get into the heavily worn front seat. The spring sticking up from the middle of the driver's seat stopped him. Next time he would make it clear that the driver's seat was to be comfortable, and the spring should stick up on the passenger's side. He was sure someone was pulling a joke on him. He actually chuckled as he folded and put his jacket over the spring.

He then got in and pushed the shiny finger polished start button. The engine started smoothly, and the purr of the engine signaled that it was tuned and in good shape. The truck might appear old, but Ian was sure it was ready to go the distance at any speed he needed to go.

The truck reminded him of the old floor shift pickup he had often driven when he was only fourteen. It had been one of the vehicles other than the tractors that he had driven as a farm boy.

Ian took his time driving down highway 3-21. He was in no particular hurry. His destination was an old, secluded farmhouse just outside of the city of Culiacan. The farmhouse had been arranged by his unseen support team. He hoped it would be as safe a location as they had promised.

Culiacan was much like Pittsburg where two rivers merge to form the Ohio River. In this case the Tamazula and Humava Rivers met to form the Culiacan River. Unlike Pittsburg, Culiacan was not as industrial.

Culiacan was home to the Sinaloa Cartel. The Cartel headquarters was about five miles away on the other side of the city. The city, the cradle of Mexican drug trafficking since the 1960s, was prospering in spite of the fact that their main official business was growing and exporting tomatoes. It was clear to Ian that more than exporting tomatoes made the local economy boom.

The city was dotted with money changing outlets, jewelry stores and luxury car showrooms. It was an accepted fact that the drug business was good for the city and a blind eye was turned to the business of the cartel. The underlining theme was to enjoy the prosperity that the gringo drug users provided.

Ian had done his homework and was aware that the Sinaloa Cartel was led by "Shorty" Guzman an exceptional leader who though currently in prison still outmaneuvered his competitors and for many years the governments that sought to shut him down. Ian was impressed with his ability to constantly adjust to the changing situation and move the Sinaloa Cartel into a more powerful position.

To Ian, it appeared that even from prison, Guzman was managing the strongest Cartel in Mexico. It had a very strong presence in the United States and across the world and had a much broader presence than the other cartels. Ian had read reports that this cartel moved up to two thirds of the drugs trafficked in the US. That was a huge advantage in terms of the resources that he could mount against his competitors.

The Cheshire moon, its smile bright in the night sky provided just enough light for Ian to see the gravel road that he was looking for.

Ian turned off the highway and followed the narrow one lane drive. It was bordered with a rusty wire fence held up by steel poles in the same rusty condition. The dry grass appearing to be a sandy tan, reflected the moonlight. The way was dotted with cactuses sporting their colorful red to purple fruit. In the night light these fruits appeared to be almost black with black flowers on top.

The stucco, single level building with a flat roof was accompanied by what Ian thought of as a small, weathered plank out building similar to a small barn he would have found back in Iowa. Both buildings had seen better days but seemed sturdy and useable.

Ian stopped and opened the double doors to the barn. After opening the doors Ian found the light switch on the beam on which the left door was mounted. The light made the roof beams of the barn appear to be the black ribs of some ancient giant beast.

He noted the bales of hay stacked to one side and the pile of loose straw just to the right of the hay.

Ian drove the pickup in and turned off the engine. He decided to unload the explosives and put them under the straw. Then he took his suitcase and backpack, closed the doors to the shed and locked it.

He walked across the drive to the house.

It was time to take a shower and get a good night's sleep. He hoped the black tank of water on the roof would provide some hot water.

The night passed uninterrupted and the morning sun stream through the bedroom window was Ian's wake up call.

Ian got up and looked to see if there was any coffee or other food in the house. Indeed, the team had provided him with coffee, eggs, sausage, and some instant oatmeal.

After a cup of coffee and breakfast, Ian drove slowly into and through Culiacan. The building cranes rising above multiple construction sites signaled a healthy economy. Ian continued out to the eastern edge of town toward the warehouse that was the regular meeting place for the cartel.

He made his way around the area to a place where a few scraggly, windblown trees created a dusty oasis with a sparse but adequate covering of grasses and a few cactuses. Ian got out and scouted out the grass covered fields that surrounded the warehouse on all sides.

He found a small depression where he would be out of sight from anyone watching from the warehouse.

Ian decided it was time to complete his tour of the city. The homes of the cartel personal were located in a northwestern suburb area named Sinaloa. These were homes that the cartel members had raised their families. This gave rise to the name for the Cartel. This was an upscale neighborhood. Ian hoped his old pickup fit the image of one of the local gardeners and grounds keepers.

After his tour, Ian stopped at a local grocery. Once he had what he thought would be sufficient food for several days he returned to the farmhouse. He scrambled some eggs and fried some sausage and onions for his lunch.

Ian spent the afternoon assembling two dozen small explosive units. He wrapped them in aluminum foil and made them look like they were traps for mice and rats. He carefully placed the radio-controlled triggering unit in one end of each block. He made additional explosive units to put in the office areas.

The next morning Ian slept in and rested. Then in the late afternoon he went back out to the depression in the grass field and got under his camouflage covering. He kept watch on the white forty-foot-high warehouse that was almost the size of a football field. It dominated the landscape and blocked out most of the green patched, mangy tan looking mountains in the distant horizon.

He had learned the cartel's schedule on the first two days. Every afternoon three white SUV's drove in and parked in front of the warehouse office building.

The arrival of the SUV's seemed to be the signal for the workers to leave. Ian counted at least a dozen people going to their cars and pickups.

Ian recognized Abelel Lambasko as one of the persons in the group. He was one of Guzman's trusted leaders.

This afternoon Ian would wait until dark and then go into the warehouse to plant his bombs. He had located the surveillance cameras mounted on the top of the warehouse and had determined the safest approach was via the truck holding area.

Ian slowly crawled through the tall grass. It took him all afternoon to get across to where the trucks were parked. He waited until he was certain everyone had left and then walked slowly to the warehouse side entrance.

Once inside the warehouse, Ian stood still for a few minutes in the eerie red darkness. Ian examined the structural beams and was pleased to discover that the bottom of the warehouse had an exterior cement lip that held the metal wall siding up against the bottom of the support I-beams. This created a perfect, out of sight, place to drop the explosive charges.

In less than ten minutes Ian had walked around the periphery of the warehouse and dropped a charge behind each support beam. The building should come straight down.

The office area was built outside of the warehouse. Ian recognized this as the greatest challenge. The fact that the office was completely dark provided Ian the chance to get in and then blind the surveillance cameras.

He put on his night vision goggles and looked up from his prone position. He found the camera above the door connecting to the warehouse. He hooded it and then went in and did the same for each camera.

Once the cameras were hooded Ian quickly planted and camouflaged each charge. He purposefully excluded the main cubical work areas near the front entrance where the common office workers were located.

He took careful inventory and inspected each charge. Ian then just as carefully un-hooded each surveillance camera and retreated out of the office area.

Ian took in a deep breath of relief once he was back into the warehouse. He paused for a moment after making sure all was set; he exited the warehouse. He carefully made his way back to the field. He paused to roll up his tarp and police the area to remove all traces of his presence.

Once back in the truck he slowly drove away in the dark.

On the following morning before lunch, he packed up all is belongings. He cleaned up the small bedroom. He folded up his bed sheets and light blanket, swept the room and took all his belongings out to the truck. He cleaned the kitchen and emptied the refrigerator into a cooler he had purchased. Everything, even the trash, went into the back of his truck.

He backed his truck out of the shed and with a broom erased his tire tracks. With a pack of sanitizing wipes Ian made a last walk-through inspection in the house and the barn. He wiped every surface he might have touched.

His support team would send a team in to clean the house, but Ian was aware that he was in the heart of one of the most thorough cartel in the world. He could not be sure the cleaners would be cartel proof. He was confident that he had erased any trace of his presence.

Once in his truck, Ian drove a small distance from the cartel warehouse and parked. He took the time to eat a sandwich before hiking to where he had a clear view of the warehouse office area.

Late in the afternoon, the white SUVs made their appearance. Ian watched as the workers walked out to their cars and the occupants of the SUVs entered the building.

Ian waited a moment and then energized his listening device located in the large main meeting room. He listened just long enough to verify it was occupied before triggering the explosions.

The back portion of the office area seemed to push the warehouse wall away into the collapsing warehouse structure. A wave of tan dust rolled away from the base of the warehouse walls and the fleet of trucks fell over like dominos. The entire structure settled down and the roof was held up by the strength of the pallet racks standing below. The sidewalls had spread like the wings of a fat bird laying on the ground.

The three white SUVs remained out front, untouched. The three drivers were standing together looking startled and pointing at the transformation happening before their eyes. Their guns were drawn as if they were going to shoot.

Ian took one last look and slowly walked back to the old truck and headed south toward Apatzingan, Michoacana.

11 La Familia Michoacana

Ian had researched the leader of La Familia, Natsario Morelo Gonzoles also known as *El Más Loco,* the crazy one. He and his leadership team all had a two-million-dollar bounty on their heads. This cartel financed politicians in their bid for election. The cartel also provided aid to the less privileged who needed help. This gave Nazario Moreno González, the Robin Hood and messianic like image among the poor and the support of many in the government.

Ian knew that this image was counterbalanced with the dozens of police officials the cartel had killed.

The police had once erroneously announced killing Moreno. Still at large *El Más Loco* was being aggressively hunted. He, however, remained in firm control of the cartel. And the cartel was fully functioning.

The twelve-hour drive from Culiacan to Apatzingan with an overnight stop in Guadalajara provided Ian with time to think through the approach he had in mind.

He did not want any close at hand encounters, but he might have to go into the office building where he thought he might find Natsario. This office building was in the heart of Apatzingán.

La Familia was integrated and influenced all elements in the state of Michoacana. It was a part of the fabric of the local business, politics, and everyday life.

Ian planned to select one family member to eliminate.

He would approach the selection in an opportunistic way. The first one he could single out would be the target.

He also knew that his action would not likely have a major impact on the cartel. They had strong family capabilities.

In Guadalajara, Ian cleared the trash and other materials from the bed of the pickup. There were two bags in the locked box in the back of the pickup. One held his clothes and the other the next weapon of choice.

The weapon was almost the identical weapon to the one he had used in Gaza. It was a high-powered sniper's rifle.

It was just past ten in the morning as Ian drove slowly along Jose Maria Morelos highway on his way into Apatzingán.

He passed the airport and wished he could catch a plane back home instead of continuing on. He missed talking to Leslie, but he could not take the chance of calling her. He knew that he needed to stay invisible.

The local traffic picked up as he turned right on Acatita and headed into Apatzingán's central district. Traffic came to a stop and Ian could see a police barricade ahead. He stopped and looked around.

He decided he would turn off and proceed on the back streets to the apartment building he had selected as a place where he could study the downtown area. It had a clear view of the downtown central park but was far enough away that he could study the downtown and not worry about being seen. There were several closer buildings, but they were occupied by business offices, and he would risk being noticed. He hoped to enter and exit the apartment building he had selected without meeting anyone.

Perhaps he would see what the police barricade was about.

The apartment building was about two blocks away from where he parked on one of the side streets. He preferred to go on foot the rest of the way. He took a moment to check out his appearance. He had whitened his hair and was wearing an old grey sports jacket and a pair of worn slacks. He wanted to appear like an old man returning home from a trip.

Ian retrieved a battered suitcase from the back of the pickup. He slowly walked up the street. He hoped anyone watching would see a worn old man carrying a battered suitcase and ignore him.

He slowly walked up the hill leading to the old apartment building. In the distance he could hear what he thought was the popping sound of gunfire. He figured that might be the reason for the police blockade.

Ian found an open side door to the apartment building. Once inside he followed the hallway to the elevators.

He entered the right-hand elevator and pushed the button with the number seventeen barely legible to the eye. The old elevator creaked and groaned as it slowly took him to the top floor.

The hallway outside of the elevator passed by a series of apartment doors. Ian went to the end of the hallway and climbed the stairs to a locked service door that led to the roof. He easily picked the lock and stepped cautiously out onto the roof.

He looked quickly around. The black tar and gravel roof was bordered by a three-foot-high red brick wall. Four large black water tanks towered above him and dominated the majority of the roof area.

The rest of the roof area had an assortment of ventilation pipes and some boxes that Ian took to be fan units. The roof was deserted, and its appearance indicated it was seldom used.

Ian locked the door and then picked up a section of pipe and propped it under the door handle to make sure it could not be opened. He did not want anyone surprising him from behind.

He then crossed to the side of the building that faced in the direction where he still periodically heard the popping of gunfire.

Ian took off his jacket, opened the suitcase and placed it carefully on the open lid.

The interior of the suitcase belied the shabby exterior. The black foam interior cradled a two-inch diameter, foot long scope with a plastic glare cover of the same length. The long slender black barrel that reminded Ian of a sleek black shark was just below it and the back end of ten six-inch-long bullets created a poke a dot brass and silver pattern below the barrel. The padded plastic stock of the rifle on the opposite side from the scope balanced the layout.

Ian carefully assembled the single fire sniper rifle. This was a gun that any NRA maniac would fall in love with. He snugged the single bolt connecting the barrel to the stock. Then he gently positioned the scope on the front and back groves and pushed it down until he felt the spring-loaded balls snap into place. The scope mounting design was one that assured the exact positioning required for extremely long shots.

Ian slowly pulled out each bullet and put them in the depressions designed into the foam rubber. The long slender six-inch-long shell with the quarter inch diameter one-inch-long bullet head always caught him by surprise. They were truly a beautiful sight that attracted him as much as any well-built bikini clad lady and he considered them even more deadly.

Ian looked up at the clear blue, cloudless sky. A gentle breeze was blowing over the wall in front of him. He located the sun, confirmed the direction of the wind, and then looked out to those structures that were higher than where he was.

Ian was now ready to look over the wall.

Out to his left and about two blocks away was a building towering above the main downtown square. There he saw two snipers with their right sides visible to him. He was not sure if there were more snipers on that roof top.

Three snipers with their backs to him were visible on two buildings in front of and slightly below his elevation. Their building seemed to overlook the town square. He wondered why they were not shooting. They had a better position than he had.

Ian completed his slow and careful scan of the entire scene surrounding the battle area in the square several blocks away.

Ian had a clear view of eight black SUV's forming a barricade on one side of the square. A series of police cars and military vehicles were on the other side of the square. The police side had many more people moving about then what Ian saw by the black vans.

The two sides appeared to be in a standoff.

Ian sat back down and put a bullet into the chamber of the rifle.

Once again Ian felt the breeze and took in the position of the sun.

This time Ian put his jacket down, so he could comfortably kneel on it while he lay the rifle barrel on the top of the wall.

He looked through his scope at the various figures crouched down behind the black SUV's. Ian could not believe it when the third figure he focused on was none other than "El Chayo," the crazy one.

This was an opportunity that could not to be denied but he was at the extreme of his sniper capability. The shot must hit the mark. He needed to calibrate his shot.

Ian took careful aim at the zero of the license plate on the SUV "El Chayo" was hiding behind. He slowly squeezed the trigger.

The hole that appeared on the license plate was two inches to the left but at the same height as his aim.

Ian made a mental aim adjustment, chambered the next bullet, took a deep breath, and found his target. He once again smoothly squeezed the trigger.

"El Chayo" seemed to look up at Ian at the moment the trigger was squeezed. After what seemed to Ian to be an eternity, a small dark spot appeared in El Chayo's forehead and a moment later he went down.

Ian did not wait but loaded and fired one bullet after the another at the row of men behind the SUV's. Each body shot found its target.

Ian saw one of the police wave to the snipers as the army and police surged across the square. Ian was sure the snipers were all surprised. They would be looking around to see where the shots had come from.

Ian sat back down behind the wall and carefully removed the scope and repacked it. He then cleaned the rifle barrel before placing it back in its place. Finally, he pushed each empty bullet casing into their holding place. He noted that the firing pin was striking slightly off center as he closed the suitcase and made a mental note to adjust it when he next used the rifle. Then he laughed as he realized he would never use it again.

After ensuring the roof area held no evidence of his presence Ian closed the door to the roof behind him.

Ian had been totally calm for the entire period on the roof. Now in the elevator, he felt nervous that everything had been too easy, too fast, and too smooth. His senses were heightened as he anticipated facing someone with a gun as he exited the building.

Ian walked slowly out of the building and back to his truck. He expected to be called out or shot at, at any moment. He put the old suitcase into the back of the pickup and got in.

He sat for a few moments before putting his finger on the start button. The engine once again began to purr like an aroused cat. He was still parked after a few moments.

He noted that he had literally just driven into Apatzingan and had accomplished his goal in less than an hour. This would most likely go down as the fastest solution on this trip.

It was time to leave the area.

12 Beltran Leyva Cartel

Ian was not sure this last target qualified as the leader of a major cartel. Four brothers originally formed the Beltran Leyva cartel when they broke away from the Sinaloa cartel after Joaquin Guzman betrayed them by turning in their oldest brother to the government. The brothers ordered the murder of Joaquin's son in retaliation and at the same time formed their own cartel.

Ian was aware that both personal dislike and business competition ruled the relationships between the cartels. The competition between the cartels provided more control and restraint of their actions than the actions by either the Mexican or US government. Each cartel monitored and pushed back on any encroachment into their territory or their market.

The Beltran Leyva cartel became known for their kidnapping, torture, and murder against various Mexican people especially Mexican law enforcement officials. This made them more of a target by the government than was exerted on the other cartels.

Even in its weakened state, the Beltran Leyva cartel was still running and distributing drugs in the US. It really was the classic story of the multi-headed snake. Cutting one head off just meant another would grow or another head would became stronger. The consumption of drugs in the US fed the various heads and US consumption of drugs was going up as the US economy got better. The market was adequate to make all the cartels rich.

Between the US and Mexican governments there was a seven million dollars bounty for the one remaining brother, Hector Beltran Leyva, "El Ingeniero", the engineer.

Ian's research indicated Hector was hiding in plain sight. He was living with an early childhood friend who had become a successful soap opera star. She was past her youthful prime but was still doing commercials on a local Mexico City television channel.

Her flat was in a very nice part of the city across the street from two prestigious hotels.

This was an affluent area of nice homes and apartments.

Ian was very familiar with the hotels and the area. This was where he stayed during his legitimate regular business trips to Mexico City.

Her apartment or condo was directly behind a Starbucks outlet across the street from the locally owned prestigious hotels, so Ian selected a room with a view of Starbucks.

From the top of the hotel, Ian could look down into the apartment pool area that was across the street behind Starbucks. He spent several days just watching the pool to see if the pool would attract his target. It would make it very easy if Hector were to come out for a swim. It was a clear and relatively easy shot from the roof.

Ian had no such luck.

Instead, Ian saw a person who took a morning walk out to Starbucks and then walked down a few blocks and back around Emilio Castelar street back to Anstotelos street and returned to the apartment building.

He was sure he had found his target. He waited and watched for another day to make certain he had found his target.

Then the following morning Ian was sitting in Starbucks when Hector came in. Hector was much thinner and trimmer than the mug shots Ian had studied or that graced the various newspapers, but Ian was certain it was "El Ingeniero."

Hector ordered a large cappuccino. Once he had been served, he left with it in hand and went for his normal walk.

Ian walked slowly in the opposite direction. He was carrying only an ink pen from the hotel room. It was all he would need.

Hector was concentrating on his coffee and his walk as Ian nodded to him and said good morning in English.

Hector nodded but didn't really pay attention. That was his last mistake.

Ian's left hand placed the pen into Hector's ear and his right hand came down like a sledge and drove it through. Ian quickly removed the pen and continued walking. He never looked back.

He walked to the hotel and went into the restroom where he washed the pen. He then went out to the lobby and distributed the pieces of the pen in the various trash receptacles.

Once back in his hotel room, Ian took a quick shower, packed his bags, and checked out of the hotel.

Ian took several taxis to get to the airport. He disposed of his remaining weapons, explosives, and other equipment each time he changed taxis. He disposed of the sniper rifle one piece at a time. He hated to destroy such a beauty but there was no other way. He had taken the time to ensure there was no remaining gun powder in the bullets he disposed of. No two component parts were disposed in the same trash container or in close proximity trash cans.

The third taxi he flagged down took him to the Airport.

The total time to get to the airport took several hours longer than normal. Once there he was able to book a flight to Dallas, Texas. In Dallas, Ian went to another airline and booked a flight home.

Ian was anxious to give Lesley a big hug.

He stopped to give her a call and let her know that he was on the way home.

Lesley knew Ian was gentle and kind in the open life he lived.

She had voiced her suspicion about the worst for the other.

Ian had never confirmed his alternate personality. He was afraid that if Lesley ever learned the truth of the actions, he perpetrated she might leave him.

All she had ever asked was if Ian was one of the good guys.

Ian had replied that he thought he was.

He hoped he was one of the good, result-oriented, problem-solvers.

He also hoped that he would not get another problem-solving assignment.

The End

Preview of: Border Crossers

<u>1 Border Crosser</u>

Ian watched as the news camera zoomed in on the back of a panel truck. It had been found by the Arizona highway patrol abandoned in the hot summer Arizona sun. The external temperature had reached an ungodly one hundred thirteen degrees.

The truck was filled with more than thirty bodies. It was clear by how they were piled up trying to scale the interior wall that the occupants had used their hands or a boot trying to break out. Ian was sure that to the end the occupants were desperately shouting, crying, and pleading to be let out. The backdoor was bent, and one occupant had broken his leg, and the bone was exposed in a grotesque angle. The hands with their fingernails ripped back clearly indicated to Ian the final desperate efforts to claw their way out.

Ian absorbed the scene as the camera pulled to a distant view and then zoomed in on a mother cradling a young girl and boy to her chest. The three seemed to be in a Cinderella sleep just waiting to wake up.

The reporter walked away with a cloth over his nose as he commented about the stench of death. Some bodies were already beginning to bloat. There seemed to be an even mix of men, women, and children. It was clear to Ian that this had been mostly family units trying to get into the US.

The woman holding her children to her chest became the focus of the reporting. The report was picked up by all the national news channels and it went viral on the personal chat sites. The picture went viral with multimillion of hits in just one evening.

Ian let out a groan when he heard a national news caster say, "We need action to be taken against those trafficking in across the border people smuggling. We especially need someone to take action against smugglers that abandon people in locked trailers." This was clearly a message for him to act. He was the problem-solver.

Ian watched several other major channels and listened to the same message. There was no doubt. The message could not have been clearer.

Ian left the grand family room. It was the place where he spent the early morning with a cup coffee and listened to Morning Joe before tuning in on BBC, CNN and then going on to Fox. He liked to keep a balanced perspective on what was being watched by the rest of the world. So much of what was presented as news was actually biased opinion by one side of the political aisle or the other.

Ian went down the hallway to his study.

He walked in and took in the book lined shelves along the two side walls of what had originally been a home library but over the years had become his office. The mahogany desk with a black three-foot-wide all in one computer faced the rear window overlooking the tennis court and the lawn around it. The Library was where he spent many hours doing research.

Ian booted up the computer and began his search on the topic of smuggling people.

After a moment he opened the bottom left hand desk drawer and extracted a locked box from the very back. He opened and picked up an older phone that did not have GPS as a function. He slowly dialed a well memorized number. It was immediately answered. He was sure the person on the phone had been expecting the call.

"Send me everything you have on smuggling people across the Mexican border. Set me up as an FBI agent with orders to go to Arizona. Give me the name of the field agent that manages that area. Arrange for me to get there in two days. And thank you," Ian said as politely as possible.

Early in his career as the problem-solver he had tried to be friendly, but he was soon calibrated on the fact that the people on the other end of the line were to remain anonymous. Whoever they were and however many made up his support team was unknown to him. He had envisioned a large work area all full of people doing his bidding and he had also envisioned a gray-haired old lady with coke bottle bifocals sitting in a darkened closet like office.

He would probably never know. All he cared about was that his support team always delivered what he needed.

The requested material began coming in almost immediately. They must have anticipated his request. He reviewed the information from past reports on the smuggling and movement of those coming across the border.

He learned of an earlier abandoned truck full of people. It had not made the news. The fact that two trucks had been abandoned in the last two months seemed to indicate carelessness, disregard or of an increased pressure by local law enforcement that frightened the drivers and caused them to abandon their trucks.

Smugglers always preferred to remain anonymous. Getting caught was their greatest fear. Subsequent publicity meant exposure and scrutiny, so their bosses were as likely to kill them as anyone.

The US border patrol preferred to keep the media at arms-length.

Inadvertently this penchant to keep press coverage low caused the police to aid the smugglers.

Ian looked up the local law enforcement officers in Phoenix. Phoenix was where the Highway Patrol, the Local county sheriff and the FBI regional offices were located.

He reviewed the background and assignments of the local FBI Phoenix office chief. He seemed to have a well-rounded background including a stint in the Army. He appeared to be a solid individual with personal integrity.

The human smugglers had to get past the security, monitoring and patrolling done by Homeland Security. In fact, the border patrol and the Homeland Security organization were highly trained and highly motivated. Ian's assessment was that they were good at their jobs. He also suspected that some of them must be part of the smuggling operation. The crossers had to get past the field teams and that indicated some sort internal agents working for the cartels.

The local sheriffs and State Highway Patrol seemed to be vigilant in their efforts to intercept the cars and truck involved in the smuggling. They seemed to focus on looking for those being smuggled. It was unlikely that they had any direct involvement, but he would at this point not rule it out.

Ian suspected that there were a few bad actors in these organizations that would cause the good side to get a black eye. He was certain that there was one or more bad apple in the local law enforcement agencies.

He listed the way people could be crossing the border and not be getting caught.

There could be participation by local law enforcement personnel. There could be a group of border guards that would look the other way. In all cases it appeared that those doing the smuggling had help on the US side of the border.

Ian knew he needed to go to the field and get firsthand knowledge to understand the true situation.

He had already asked for his FBI persona to be reactivated. He was Herman A. Lunquist, senior FBI investigator.

Ian reviewed his past history as Herman. It had continued to be updated and he laughed about some to the compliments and his high work evaluations. Someone on his support team was having a good time fabricating and building his history.

He had many personalities on record but only a few got reactivated as often as Herman. For his Journey into Russia, he had become a naturalist. In taking care of the Three Bad Pennies, he had become a cameraman.

This was a natural build because he had taken on the role of a cameraman on a team of National Geographic photographers out to document the Elephant Ivory trade plight. For fighting the Pirates off the coast of Africa he had become a sailboat captain.

Ian let Lesley know that he had an upcoming business trip out west. She immediately knew what kind of business and as always gave him a kiss on the cheek and told him to be careful. Over the years Lesley had come to accept the fact that Ian would remain a problem-solver for most of his life. She constantly reminded him that they had the small fortune most people dreamed of having.

Ian gave her a hug and thanked her for loving him.

Herman Lundquist had a high status as an FBI agent. He called Mike Lancaster the local FBI branch manager, Mike had agreed to meet him at the airport and escort him to the local FBI office.

As he came to the end of the concourse and walked out of the security area Ian spotted Mike almost immediately. Mike was roughly six two with dark hair cut almost in a short military style.

Ian put him in the handsome category and thought he could have starred in the movie, Men in Black.

Ian could tell that Mike was nervous and probably wondering why he, a senior FBI investigator, was there. In the car on the way to the office Ian explained that he had been sent to work with Mike because the FBI hierarchy was feeling pressure about the fact that two loads of people had died in the back of trucks and there seemed to be no solution in stopping it.

Mike thanked Ian for clarifying his presence and that he could see the reason he had been sent. He wondered what Ian was going to do.

The FBI office was in the local Federal building in the heart of downtown Phoenix.

On their way up from the basement parking lot, Mike informed Ian that an office had been arranged for him and that they would share Mary Gems as their secretarial support.

They approached Mary's desk where Mike introduced Ian.

After some small talk and asking about her family, Ian asked if she would set up breakfast or lunch meetings with the leaders of the Highway Patrol, the Sheriff's office, and the Homeland Security Leader.

Ian made the point that he wanted his meetings to be on an informal basis. He did not want formality to become a barrier. He wanted everyone to know him on a more personal basis and feel somewhat relaxed around him.

Mary agreed to do so but made the point that the Homeland Security Leader was located in a small town about two hours away.

He suggested that meeting be arranged to meet the Homeland Security Leader's timing.

Mike next led Ian to an office next to his.

Ian commented that he hoped not to be at the desk at all.

Next Mike walked to a small room with a coffee pot, a shelf full of cups, a small refrigerator and stainless-steel sink.

"This is as good as it gets here in the office. If you want something better, May's restaurant just down the street makes a great breakfast and lunch and serves a variety of soft drinks, iced tea as well as great cup of coffee," Mike fired off in rapid order.

Ian could tell that Mike was still nervous.

He had a good feeling about Mike. He could see them working well together.

Ian followed Mike out of the coffee room

He asked Mike to bring him up to date on the investigation of the deaths of the people found in both of the abandoned panel trucks.

Mike said that the trucks were registered to two separate local truck rental companies. The rental companies had contracts on file for the trucks and everything was in order. The persons renting the trucks and their driver license information were fake. Both rentals led nowhere.

The FBI was working with the state and states around to see if they could determine who the drivers might have been. The trail at this moment was cold.

The records of the companies were being reviewed to determine how many other times a truck had been rented under a fictitious name. The net had been cast wider and truck rentals from all rental companies were being scrutinized.

Mike commented that it would take time to get through this investigation.

Ian commented on the impressive and solid approach Mike was pursuing. He went on to describe how great it would be if the two of them solved this current case and put an end to trucks being abandoned.

He asked Mike to speculate what action he would take if he could take any action he wanted. What would he do?

There was a soft knock on the door just as Mike was about to answer. Mary opened the door and informed them that she had set up breakfasts for the next three days for the two of them.

Ian thanked Mary and she closed the door.

He then suggested that he and Mike continue their discussion over lunch.

Mike led the way to May's. He said that he recommended the Reuben special.

After lunch Mike dropped him off at the downtown hotel.

Ian checked in and went up to his room. After a long shower, he sat down and turned on his computer and thoroughly reviewed the information he had on each of the law enforcement leaders.

Mathew Martin was the leader of the highway patrol. In his mid-fifties Mathew had served in the Marines. He had a wife and three children, all now in their late teens and early twenties. He had an impressive record and had quickly risen in the state's highway patrol organization. It made no sense to Ian that he would be involved.

Bill Peters was the local sheriff. He too had the same family profile. He had an Army background and had been elected sheriff four times. He was known for his active participation in getting downtown Phoenix renovated and well-lit, so people could safely enjoy their time in the city.

It made no sense to Ian that either these two would be involved.

He, however, did not rule out someone in their organization.

The next morning, he walked to May's diner. The appealing smell of fresh rolls, bacon and was trumped by the smell of coffee. As the waitress poured his coffee it immediately captured Ian's mind and made his stomach growl. He sat down and looked around. He had arrived early, so he could watch the customers come in.

Someone in a dark blue city police uniform with a gold badge on the chest came in and sat in a far corner booth. A moment later a person in a tan uniform with State Highway Patrol embroidered where the sleeves met the shoulder came in and joined the person in the corner. They both looked over at Ian.

Ian took in the two seasoned, well-aged older men sitting in full uniform at the booth. He stood and walked over and introduced himself. He had planned to meet first with the highway patrol leader, but it was clear they had talked to each other.

The Highway Patrol leader introduced himself as Mathew Martin and then introduced the City Police Chief, Bill Peters.

Mathew said he preferred to be called Matt, said that the two had talked and decided that they would meet the investigating FBI leader together.

Ian thanked them for having breakfast with him.

At that moment Mike walked in and came over to the table. He apologized for being late.

Ian noted that Mike seemed to be treated as one of them.

Ian was the odd one out and was the one they all seemed to be wondering about. He surprised the group by asking about their families and the age of their kids. He had the statistics of each family, but he was interested in listening to how each of the people at the table related to their family.

The discussion that followed made it clear to him that "Matt" and Bill were old and good friends. He made note that these were family men, proud of their work and solid in their integrity. This made it easier for Ian. If there was corruption in their organization, it would involve those below these two. The problem would be deeper in the organization, but he would not be fighting the organization leaders.

After breakfast, Ian accompanied by Mike went on tour of the border and to the office of border security to see how they operated.

The drive to the office of border security took over an hour. Ian used this time to get to know Mike. He listened as Mike described coaching his two sons in soccer, baseball, and basketball. Mike did not want his sons to play football.

They arrived at the Homeland Security office and met with Ricard Butterfield the regional director. Rick, as he wanted to be called, showed Ian a map and the way the area was patrolled. He invited Ian on a drive through tour along the border.

Ian gladly accepted. Rick led the way to a large, air-conditioned trail buggy and for the rest of the day he, Mike and Rick drove the route that his border guards patrolled.

It didn't take Ian long to figure out that the guys in the field needed directions from the drones that flew overhead.

They and their dogs made great teams. The dog handlers all took to Ian once their dogs allowed Ian to scratch them behind their ears. Their dogs showed them that Ian was OK. They commented that Ian was one of a handful of people that the dogs accepted.

Ian laughed and replied that his wife thought he was a dog too.

The team described how they went about their normal daily patrol. Their manner was professional, thorough, and very conscientious.

After learning about how the field teams were guided, Ian asked to tour the drone control office and understand how they interacted with the ground team.

Rick said the tour would need to be the next day around noon. He was joining Matt and Joe for his usual midweek breakfast at May's. He asked whether Mike would be there.

Mike answered in the affirmative and looked at Ian to see what his response would be.

Ian answered that he wouldn't miss it.

The next day after breakfast Mike and Ian followed Rick back to the Border Patrol offices. Rick led the way in and walked Ian and Mike through the normal observation shift and the communication with the border patrol vehicle surveillance and the dog patrol teams.

It was clear the drone handlers had the best vantage point to see almost everything. A mole on this team could easily provide the information that would misdirect those on the ground.

On the drive back, Ian asked Mike to check on the background of all the drone operators.

Ian again guided the conversation to Mike and his family.

Mike described his home as strategically located between the Middle School, where his youngest son and middle daughter attended, and the High school where his oldest son was now in his junior year.

The family Church was just beyond the middle school. The family doctor was located across from the High School and a hospital was just a stone's throw north of the high school.

He and his wife belonged to a health club less than three miles away. Mike described it as a convenient arrangement for the family.

He had a large two story, five-bedroom home on a corner lot that faced third street and was blessed with a dead-end street to its right.

Mike made a point of mentioning the nine-foot interior ceilings that kept the air conditioning bill reasonable. He liked the fact that the large size of the house and the relatively small size of the lot which made the yard work reasonably easy.

Mike extended an invitation to Ian to a family grill out. He explained the grilling would happen out in the backyard, but everyone would be taking shelter in the air-conditioned back patio.

Ian said he would love to meet his family and looked forward to the grill out.

Ian spent Saturday sleeping in late, taking a swim and working out. He took in a movie and spent some time reviewing the case.

Sunday morning early Ian took a walk-through downtown Phoenix. The heat of the day was building when he flagged down one of the few cabs and gave him Mike's address.

The grill out and meeting the family put Ian in a good mood. Then toward the end of the day Mike received a call. He beckoned Ian over and quietly shared the fact that the border patrol had lost a large group of border crossers but had seen a light grey or perhaps dirty white panel truck leaving the area.

Ian and Mike agreed to skip the Monday breakfast and meet early in the office and figure out what to do.

That evening Ian began to study the routes that he would choose if he were transporting illegal aliens and wanted to minimize his chances of getting caught.

Based on the mileage of each of the two confiscated trucks that had been previously used Ian plotted various routes. He decided to check these routes with Matt and Bill at breakfast on Monday morning.

Ian met Mike at the office and suggested that they have breakfast at Mays. He had questions for both Bill and Matt.

Mike was especially interested in Ian's study on possible travel routes and wondered why his team had not done something similar.

Ian pointed out that he had no clue about travel in the region, but he didn't know what else to do so he was doing what he always did best. He created his own sandbox to play in and hoped there was no cat shit in it.

There seemed to be one route that best fit the miles. It also ended just shy of Interstate 40, which was a main East-West traffic corridor. Ian had used a red pen to trace Highway 80 north, to 75, to 78, to 180 then on to 32, 36 and finally 117. This brought both trucks very close to Interstate 40. It was a slow tedious route, but it certainly kept the trucks off the main thoroughfares.

Ian figured that it was probably around this area where a transfer to other modes of transport would be made. The second leg could be many via separate transports. There were endless dispersal scenarios that Ian could think of.

Matt and Bill concurred on the route Ian liked best. They figured it was as good as any and asked what good knowing this would now do for those who had died.

Ian agreed that it did nothing for them, but he felt it might help to be ready for the next time. And he pointed out that Rick had let Mike know on Sunday that a white panel truck had left the border.

Ian decided to drive and feel out the route he had mapped. He figured his chances were very low of finding anything, but the drive would occupy him and give him time to decide on the next steps he needed to take.

He asked Mike if the office kept any cases of water handy and found out that indeed they had extra cases on hand. He asked that several cases be put in the trunk.

Mike said he would have one of his guys put it in the back of the car Ian was being issued and asked if Ian was expecting to find a truck load of people.

Ian replied that he had no clue, but he was going to be Boy Scout ready.

Ian walked out to the assigned car, checked the trunk, and threw in his small personal needs bag.

Ian left Phoenix and began what he decided was a scenic drive through the scraggly pine covered mountains surrounded by a wide skirt of sage, cactus and tumble weed stretch of barren desert. Ian encountered almost no traffic. An occasional car or truck going the opposite direction broke the otherwise monotonous drive. He was almost all the way to Interstate 40 when a white panel truck stopped on the side of the road caught his eye. He slowed down as he drove past.

He saw no one.

The truck seemed to be deserted. A red flag went up in Ian's shocked mind. Unbelievably it was the exact scenario he had imagined.

Ian decided to go back to the truck and take a closer look. He parked just past the truck on the opposite side of the road and carefully approached the truck. He looked out to the right of the truck to see if the driver was out in that direction. The underside of the truck was clear. It seemed the truck was deserted.

Ian walked up to the cab and stepped up on the sideboard to look in.

Almost immediately there was pounding on the panels from inside the back of the truck. He walked to the back of the truck. The doors were locked.

Ian pounded on the backdoor and in Spanish he told them to wait a moment. He would open the back doors.

The truck had a cross lug nut wrench but no straight bar. Ian went to his car and came back with the hockey stick style lug wrench most cars carry. The lock was a standard case quarter inch shank. It snapped on his first hard twist.

A swoosh of hot air from inside hit him as the doors came open. Ian was almost overwhelmed by the smell of sweat and urine. He was immediately angered by these conditions. The relief of finding everyone alive was the only thing that placated Ian.

The people inside needed help and they needed water. Ian knew that his earlier premonition that caused him to ask for the two cases of water now confirmed why he was still alive today.

He always seemed to have these premonitions.

Ian passed the water out and told everyone to drink slowly so they would not be sick.

He got everyone out and had them sit in the shade of the truck.

Ian saw a white van approaching slowly from the direction of Interstate 40. He took a bottle of water and went to the front of the panel truck. He stood leaning against the front of the truck. The heat of the radiator added to the heat of the sun.

The oncoming van stopped about twenty feet from the truck. Two men with guns drawn got out and approached him.

They asked what the hell Ian was doing letting the people out of the truck.

Ian calmly told them to take it easy and that he had stopped to see if he could help. Ian pointed to the engine compartment. He told them that he was a mechanic in Phoenix and just happened to be driving by. Ian went on to claim that he had fixed hundreds of engines of this type and that he could help them.

The taller of the two said they would fix their own truck and Ian should just get on his way.

Ian took note that the group along the side of the truck were now standing and quietly watching. The group seemed to distract the two gunmen.

The two had finally reached the distance when Ian could go into action. He waited until the two took their next step forward.

The taller of the two took the step forward that Ian had been waiting for. Ian threw his water bottle at him and took a long step forward. He deflected the gun hand with his left hand while at the same time stepping down hard on the arch of his right foot. He kept the gunman's body between him and his partners. The final stiff finger stab to his throat took him down.

As the taller gunman was just beginning to crumble, Ian delivered a round house kick to the second gunman's temple area and followed it with a downward fist blow to his nose. The second gunman fell down on his knees holding his nose with two hands and then toppled over.

Ian quickly picked up the two guns and checked the two for any other weapons. Both were carrying hunting style knives.

Ian threw the knifes back to the on-looking crowd.

He asked the on lookers to take off the men's boots and pants and to throw them both into the back of the truck.

Ian was surprised by the energy and enthusiasm the crowd displayed as they picked the two up and took off the articles Ian had specified. They literally threw them into back of the truck. There was a cheer when the doors were shut.

Ian would interrogate the two but first he had to disperse the people that were now looking to him for guidance.

Thank you for reading this far.

Go to: https://www.remwriter95.net/

To read the rest of the; **Border Crosser**

About the Author

Ronald E. Mueller
remwriter95@gmail.com

Ron grew up in what is now Flint River State Park in Southeast Iowa. The 170-year-old house Ron lived in is built into a hillside. It faces a 125-foot-high cliff towering over the little Flint River. The house and the land talked to him about; the passing of time, the struggle to conquer the land, the struggles people faced and the wonder of nature.

He climbed the cliffs, crawled into the caves, dove from the swimming rock, collected clams from the bottom of the pond, gigged and skinned frogs for their legs. He trapped muskrats for fur, hunted raccoon in the dead of night, and with only a stick hunted rabbits in the dead of winter.

His young life was outdoors, and nature tested him.

He walked to a one room stone schoolhouse uphill both ways. A stern but warm-hearted teacher, Mrs. Henry was instrumental in shaping his character as she shepherded him from the fourth to the eighth grade.

It was a great way to grow up.

Ron graduated from Burlington, High School, went to Vietnam in the Navy. He graduated from The University of South Florida with a master's degree in engineering, worked for thirty eight years for Procter and Gamble, traveled around the world thirty times.

He has remained happily married for more than fifty years. His daughter and his two sons are all successful and his three grandchildren have all graduated.

His wife has humored and supported him as he became a full time professional story teller.

He has come to realize that he is, what is known as, a Cozy writer. Excitement and adventure but little guts and gore. His heroine or hero suffer a little but live happily ever after.
His experiences inter-twined with snippets of fantasy lend themselves to the adventures he leads the reader through.

Books by the Author

Fiction Series

The Alex Evercrest Series
The River Front
The Girl on The Grill
Missing
Maggot
Racist
Votive Candles
Windy City
Country Road
Pool of Blood
Sins of the Daughter
Body Parts
The Skull Collector
The Vanishing
The Shadow Fighter
Moonshine
Grief's Trajectory
The Magic Touch
Northern Lights
Alex Evercrest Heroine
Alex Evercrest Collection Two
New Direction
A Family Affair
Disruption
Aftermath
The St. Lebuinnus Church Murder

A Brian O'Neil Novel
Hawaiian Phoenix
Moon Curser
Death Broker

The Problem Solver Series
Solutions
Drug Lords
Border Crosser
The Problem Solver Collection

The Taelo Series
The Early Years
The Golden Feather
Journey of Discovery
Dangerous Passage
Condor Clan Slingers
Circumvention
The Journey of Sages
Collection
Future Leaders Journey

<u>**A Taelo Story:**</u>
White Swan and Quiet Pheasant
The Child's Name
Floating Cloud
Quiet Rabbit
Busy Bee
Little Otter & Talking Wren
Broken Spear
Burley Bear & Meadow Flower
Taelo Story Collection

Science Fiction

<u>The Savitar Series:</u>
Journey's End
Savitar
Confluence
Savitar Series Collection

<u>The Door Series</u>
The Door
Aliens We
The Endless Hole
The Swarm
Esoteric Journey
The Gentle Eye
The Door Series Collection

<u>Bram Nielson Series</u>
The Fold
The Message
Fold Wormhole
Negative Fold
Ripples in Time
Bram Nielson Collection

<u>Single Science Fiction Books:</u>
Current Past and Future
The Event
The Door
Viajante 7

Published by: Around the World Publishing LLC.